Hidden Lake

By Linda Pratt

Contents

Chapter 1

Gruff Hammer jumped the fence and raced toward the treasure chest at the far end of the forest. If he could get there before Swamp Beast, he would have enough poison darts to destroy all the Retch Demons in Sector Eight.

Seth Bowman worked his smart phone feverishly, focused on the characters on the screen as the Montana countryside whizzed by his car window. At 14, he was all knees and elbows, with a shock of dark chocolate hair that tended to hang in his eyes. His brown eyes sparked as another Retch Demon fell back and dissolved into a gray-green mist.

"Ok, put it away," said his mother. "You'll have plenty of time to play at Gran and Gramps' house." Her strawberry blonde ponytail brushed the headrest as she looked back and forth between Seth and the road ahead. "Be sure to clean up after yourself and help around the house. Don't make Gran and Gramps do everything for you." She flicked on the blinker and turned right onto what seemed to be more of a path than a road.

"Are you sure this is the right way?" Seth asked. He had visited his grandparent's house once for the Christmas holidays, but he had slept most of the way.

"Uh huh," his mother said, as the tires threw up clouds of dust. "You sure you don't want to spend the summer in Europe with Mel and me?"

Seth shook his head and squinted out the window. They had been through this a dozen times. No. He did not want to watch his mom and her new husband make googly eyes at each other all summer while he tried to order something from the menu that wasn't weird or gross.

He had only been five the day his father put on his hard hat, said, "See you later, Squirt," and walked out the door never to return. The grownups around him had whispered the words "terrible accident," but he had not understood what it meant to die. For months he expected his father would one day burst through the door again to tell a story in his booming voice that only he would laugh at. Then one day, Seth realized his dad was not coming home again – ever.

Worse than never seeing his dad again, was watching the change in his mother. The corners of her mouth turned down, and she always seemed tired. Then, one day after school, as he threw his backpack on the kitchen table, his mom introduced him to a tall, skinny man with wild red hair. To Seth, it looked as if the man had a giant orange steel wool pad glued to the top of his head.

"This is Mel," his mom said.

Mel shook his hand. Seth liked that. He hated it when men rubbed his hair or punched him in the arm.

"Nice to meet you," Mel said.

Mom's smile was a little too bright. Seth realized Mel was here on *approval*. He hoped his mom realized no one else would ever be his dad. But if the man with Brillo-Pad hair made her happy, that was fine with him.

Seth's ears popped at the high altitude as the red Prius turned onto a winding drive crunching gravel under the tires. A weathered mail box with the letters "B-O-W-M-A-N" on the side stood guard in front of a large white clapboard house with black shutters and a wraparound porch.

Unfolding his legs, Seth opened the passenger door to the smell of a thousand Christmas trees. He stood up and brushed the crumbs of several hours' worth of snacks from his jeans and stretched the kinks out of his arms. He reached back and lifted his backpack from the front seat.

Instantly, an animal Seth thought might be a dog, pinned him to the side of the car. It had angry red welts on its head and a ragged stump where its left ear should have been. Baggy pouches hung below watery eyes and drool dripped off saggy jowls onto Seth's T-shirt.

"Riley, get down!" a gruff voice ordered. A red and black plaid flannel shirt that smelled of soap and bacon wrapped him in a hug. Seth looked up into a broad, grizzled face with nut brown eyes and short white hair standing straight up above chaotic gray eyebrows.

"Oh Clint, you're going to squeeze the stuffing out of him!" said a wobbly voice at his side. "Let me see!"

Seth turned and looked down at a short, plump woman with green eyes twinkling above a wide wrinkled smile. Strands of gray hair sprang from under her wide-brimmed hat like frayed rope.

She held him out from her as if she was examining a dress she was considering buying. "My but you've sprouted a good foot or two. What have you been feeding him, Maggie?"

Seth thought grownups always said things like that when they didn't know what else to say. He was tall, though – taller than most of the kids in his eighth-grade school class.

His mother clicked the trunk release and came around the car to hug his grandparents and lift Seth's bag from the back. Gramps picked up the suitcase while Seth's mom slammed the trunk shut.

"Thanks so much for letting Seth stay with you for the summer," she said. "He's really good at helping with dishes and laundry." She gave Seth a meaningful look.

As they made their way to the house, Riley ran circles around them, nearly tripping Seth and flicking everyone with his powerful tail. The tawny dog pushed vigorously against Seth's legs and thighs with its flat nose.

Dozens of colorful flowers waved cheerfully in front of the porch and massive tree branches swayed above them as Seth and his family tramped up the wooden steps. A porch swing with faded yellow pillows creaked slightly in the breeze in front of a wide window as Gramps opened the squeaky screen door and stood aside to let Gran, Maggie and Seth inside.

The smell of wood smoke filled Seth's nostrils as he stepped through the front door and waited for his eyes to adjust to the inside light. A clock ticked lazily on the mantel of a fireplace hugging one wall with two hulking brown chairs and a yellow and orange flowered couch facing it. An oval rug that looked as if were made of colorful coils of rope covered the floor.

"Up the stairs and to the left," Gramps said, handing Seth his bag and pointing to a staircase on the right. "Bathroom's at the end of the hall."

Seth took his bag and trudged up the wooden stairs with Riley at his heals, his steps echoing through the house. He opened the first door on the left to a whoosh of lavender and lemon. Dropping his bag inside the door, he glanced around. A quilt with flowered squares stretched out on top of a narrow bed with brass poles rising up from the end to form a headboard.

Riley pushed by him and strutted proudly around the room, his toe nails clicking on the smooth floor planks.

Seth walked to a small window framed with blue and white checkered curtains and looked out. Below was a shed about the size of Mom's Prius with a dozen or so chickens pecking the ground in a wire enclosure.

He turned to survey the rest of the room. A closet door stood open next to a small dresser on the wall opposite the bed. He stepped into the closet. An old rain coat hung abandoned on a hanger. Some boxes and a gold trophy squatted in a row on a shelf above the coat next to several books. He reached up and took down the trophy.

"Brad Bowman, 1st place All-State wrestling tournament," he read out loud.

Riley scratched under the bed and came out with a chewed tennis ball in his mouth. He dropped it at Seth's feet and sat back expectantly.

Seth eyed the slobbery ball. "Ew," he said.

Ignoring the ball, he flopped onto the bed and pulled out his phone. He eagerly pushed the "on" button and waited, his eyes glued to the screen.

The words "No signal" appeared in glowing letters.

"Huh?" He pressed the reset button. How could there be no internet? He turned the phone off and on again.

"I'm going now, Seth," his mother called up to him, "Come give me a hug."

Seth sighed and shoved the phone into his pocket. He pounded down the stairs with Riley following behind.

Maggie pulled him into a hug. "Remember to help Gran and Gramps, 'kay?"

He nodded and followed her out onto the porch.

"Love you," she said.

"Love you too, Mom."

He watched her climb into the car and drive out of sight.

Silence cascaded down around him. He looked up and down the road. There were no other houses in sight and no sounds of traffic. His grandparents really did live out in the middle of nowhere.

He heard a *thunk* and turned to find Riley, who had followed him onto the porch standing next to the tennis ball, watching him with eager eyes.

Trying to pick up the ball without touching the slobber, Seth raised it over his head and threw it across the road.

Riley bolted after the ball as Seth wiped his hand on his pant leg. Then he opened the door and went in, letting the screen slam behind him.

Gran came out of a door on the other side of the front room wiping her hands on her apron. "Would you like some cookies and milk?" she asked.

"Sure." said Seth.

He followed her into a bright kitchen with red rooster potholders hanging from a hook by the stove. Gramps was already sitting at a heavy wood table eating a large cookie.

"Your Gran makes the best chocolate chip cookies in the county," he said, taking another big bite. A plate piled high with cookies sat in the middle of the table.

Seth threw himself on the nearest chair and reached for one of the cookies. Mmm. They were soft and warm. Gran placed glasses of ice-cold milk in front of Seth and Gramps and then sat down, helping herself to one of the fist-sized cookies. Riley pushed through a doggy door behind Gran and appeared beside Seth's chair. Dropping the tennis ball, the dog fixed his eyes on the cookie in Seth's hand and tilted his head.

"Chocolate's not good for dogs, Riley," Gran said, "Stop begging."

Riley lay down and put his head on his paws with a disgusted snort, but his eyes never left the cookie in Seth's hand.

As the taste of chocolate filled Seth's mouth, he asked, "Where is the best place to get the internet around here?"

"You need a net?" asked Gramps.

Seth shoved another bite into his mouth, and said around it, "For playing games and texting your friends." He pulled out his phone. "You know the *internet*."

His Grandparents looked at him as if he'd spoken Swahili.

"We can look in the attic and see if we can find something you can use," Gramps ventured.

Seth gave a short laugh. "No, Gramps, the internet from a signal tower so you can use your cell phone."

"We don't have a tower like that around here that I know of, but you are welcome to use our phone anytime," answered Gramps. He pointed to a toaster-sized box hanging on the wall.

"That small square thing is a telephone?" asked Gran as she stared at his cell phone.

Seth moved over by Gran and held out his phone. "See, you push that button and you can text your friends, or play a game, get your email…download apps."

"Apps?"

"Uh huh, but right now we can't do any of those things because we don't have an internet signal. See?" He showed her the offending words, "No Signal" lighting up the screen.

"Well, maybe there is a tower like that around here somewhere," said Gramps. How about you and Riley take a walk up the road a bit and see what you can find."

"Supper's at 6:00," said Gran, as she stood and picked up Seth's empty glass.

Seth hesitated. He used his phone to tell the time.

"When the sun touches the tops of the tallest trees, head on back, OK?" said Gramps.

Seth nodded. "Sure Gramps. Thanks for the cookies Gran."

Seth followed Riley along the dirt road in front of his grandparents' house. The dog ran ahead and disappeared over a rise, only to return moments later as if to see what was keeping him. Seth kicked a rock and tried to wrap his mind around the fact that not only did Gran and Gramps not have internet, they hadn't even *heard* of it!

Chapter 2

Something wet and slimy licked Seth's ear. "Huh?" he said sleepily. He opened his eyes and saw Riley's nose inches from his face. "Ugh, Riley. Go away!" He turned and pulled the flowered quilt over his head. The dog pawed at the bedding and panted, looking for an opening in the covers.

"Fine. I'm up," Seth said, at last, throwing back the quilt. Riley jumped up and gave Seth's face another sloppy taste with his tongue. "Geez! Riley! Gross!" Seth crossed his arms in front of him.

"Breakfast's ready!" called Gran's voice. "Come and get it!" The smell of bacon floated up the stairs.

Seth checked his T-shirt and jeans. He rubbed at the spot of spaghetti sauce on the shirt from last night's dinner and decided his clothes were still clean enough to wear. He pulled on his Nikes and jumped down the stairs two at a time.

In the kitchen, Gramps sat at the table studying a reel on a fishing pole with a tackle box in front of him. Another rod leaned against the wall behind him. Gran stood by the stove, turning the bacon over in a frying pan and stirring some scrambled eggs.

"How did you sleep?" she asked.

Seth had laid awake far into the night listening to the creaks and groans of a strange house, but he answered, "Fine."

A plate of pancakes, squares of butter, and a pitcher of syrup sat in the center of the table. Mmmm. His stomach growled. His Mom usually didn't have time to cook like this. At home, he had his choice of cold cereals for breakfast.

Gramps clicked the reel. "I thought you might like to go fishing today." He cut the line with a pocketknife. "Course, the fish usually like their breakfast before this, but we might catch a late riser." He winked.

He set aside the fishing rod as Gran added a plate of bacon and a bowl of scrambled eggs to the table and sat down. After the three bowed their heads for a prayer of thanks, she said, "You boys be sure to bring home some nice trout we can fry up for supper tonight."

Seth had never been fishing, and the thought of spending a whole day holding a pole out over the water sounded awful. Still, what was he going to do all day if he didn't go? And maybe there would be signal out on the road or at the lake.

When Seth could not fit one more bite into his stomach, Gramps jerked his head toward the back door. "Ready?" he asked. He smiled eagerly at his grandson.

"Sure," said Seth as he bolted the last of his milk.

The garage door screeched as Gramps lifted it up over his head. Inside sat and old faded pick-up truck that looked as if it had once lost a fight with a sledgehammer. Seth wasn't sure what color it was.

Gramps tossed the fishing gear into the back and opened the driver's side door. Riley bounded up and planted himself in the passenger seat. Seth opened the passenger door and pushed his way onto the seat as the dog searched the boy's shirt for left-over breakfast crumbs.

"Ugh, Riley your breath stinks!" Seth pushed the dog's head away and slammed his door as Gramps turned the key and the engine growled to life.

They jerked forward, causing Seth's head to spring back and forth like a bobble-head doll. The ruts in the dirt road slapped the truck from side to side as an occasional boulder threw them up and down in quick succession. Seth pushed his hand into the ceiling to brace himself against the shaking and bouncing of the truck. At every turn, Riley leaned into Seth's shoulder, leaving snot behind.

After a half hour of jostling, the gears gave a final groan and the truck skidded to a stop.

"Oof," grunted Seth, as he opened the door and Riley bounded over him, stabbing his paws into his thighs.

Seth slid to the ground as Gramps gathered the gear from the back.

"Only a little farther to Hidden Lake, the best fishing hole this side of Denver!" Gramps handed one of the poles to Seth and pointed at the suggestion of a trail on the ground in between some bushes.

Riley dashed ahead and Gramps followed him, pushing aside tree limbs. Seth followed them as swinging branches sprang back into his face. Just when he was thinking about going back to the truck, he stepped out next to a shining lake with soft waves lapping at the shore.

He took a deep breath and shaded his eyes from the sun reflecting off the water. Patches of yellow and blue flowers grew around rocks and boulders like tiny colorful stars.

Seth filled his lungs with the sweet fresh air.

Gramps set the tackle box down by a large boulder and turned to size Seth up. "Ever been fishing before?" he asked.

Seth shook his head.

"Alright," Gramps said. "Take the pole in your right hand like this – You right-handed?"

Seth nodded.

"Hold your pole like this." He demonstrated with his own pole. "Now, see this lever?" He pointed to a thin, curved bar on the reel. "Hold it down while you flick the line out, then let it out over the water. See?" He tossed the line out in a perfect arch. It sailed out and plopped into the water.

Seth held the pole awkwardly in his hand as he clicked back the little bar and held it. Then, holding his breath, he lifted the pole high, and flicked it. The pole jerked forward, but the line snagged the branch of the tree behind him.

"Timing," said Gramps, as he pried the line loose. "Wait a bit longer before letting go."

Seth sighed. He pulled the pole back and flicked it over his head again. This time, the hook swung forward and caught in the shoulder of his shirt.

Gramps let out a whoop. "Whoa! Hold on there." He pulled a pair of pliers out of the tackle box and worked the hook out.

Seth groaned as the next cast splashed into the water at his feet.

"Better," said Gramps. "Lift your thumb just as you point the pole that way." He pointed over the lake.

Fighting the urge to the throw the entire fishing pole into the water, Seth took a deep breath and closed his eyes. He tried again. This time the line went sailing a few feet into the lake.

"I did it!" He grinned.

"Ok. Now reel it in like this," Gramps said. He clicked his own reel and quickly wound up the line.

After Seth reeled in a few casts, Gramps nodded approvingly. "Alright. I think you're ready for some bait." He sat down on the boulder and lifted a white plastic container out of the tackle box. Opening the lid, he fished in the dirt and pulled a long squirming worm. He held it out to Seth.

Seth gulped and held out his hand. When Gramps placed the wet, slimy creature in his palm, his first reaction was to dump the nasty thing onto the ground and wipe his hand on the front of his shirt. Instead, he swallowed and held it there, not sure what to do.

Gramps took out another worm. "Wrap it around your hook like this." He wrapped his worm several times around his hook, pushing the hook through the worm's middle each time.

Seth gritted his teeth. He was beginning to wish he had gone to Europe with his mom. He squinted and tried to copy what Gramps had done, but as soon as he let go of the worm, it fell into the dirt at his feet.

"You'll get the hang of it," said Gramps. He picked up the worm and neatly bated Seth's hook. Then he smiled and moved a few feet away from Seth before casting his own line far out into the water with a *plop*.

Seth pulled back his arm back and let it fly forward. The line went over the lake and splashed into the water a few feet away. At least it was in the lake and not in his shirt, he thought. He and Gramps stood quietly watching their lines cut through the ripples on the lake.

"Where's Riley?" asked Seth, looking around.

"Chasing a squirrel or rabbit, I expect," said Gramps.

"So, what happened to him?"

"You mean, why is he so confounded ugly? Or why is he all scarred up?"

Seth laughed. "Both, I guess."

Gramps squinted into the sun. "Well, only his momma knows why she chose such an ugly dog to be his papa but getting chewed up as a puppy didn't help." He jerked his pole up. "Missed him." He started reeling in. "If you feel a nibble, give a tug to set the line. I think that one might have gotten a free lunch."

Seth stared at the place where his line entered the water. He wouldn't know a nibble from a shark bite.

Gramps reeled in his line and frowned at his empty hook. As he pulled another worm out of the plastic container, he said, "There's a bunch of trouble makers down the mountain who were fighting dogs a couple years back. They train their dogs to be killers by putting puppies in the pit with them and letting the fighters tear them up. That way the fighting dog gets a taste for blood." He cast his line neatly back into the middle of the lake.

"One night I was in town getting a few supplies," Gramps continued. "I was coming out of Wally's Groceries and loading up my truck when I heard a whimpering sound."

Seth forgot about his pole and stared at Gramps.

"I followed the sound to the dumpster in the back ally. There were several small animals in it. All of them chewed up. All dead." A muscle worked in his jaw. "Except one puppy which was barely alive and just lay there crying."

"So that's what happened to his ear," said Seth.

"Yep," said Gramps. "The vet stitched him up as best as she could, but she couldn't save the ear. It was weeks before we knew for sure he was even going to make it."

As if on cue, at that moment, Riley came out of the bushes with a stick in his mouth. Dropping it at Seth's feet, he sat back on his haunches and panted eagerly.

"He really likes to fetch," said Seth, reaching down a hand to take the stick.

"Yeah. One time I kept throwing and throwing, just to see which of us would tire first." Gramps let out a little more line. "I gave up after two hours."

Seth smiled and threw the stick into the bushes.

Just then, his pole bobbed.

"You got one!" said Gramps. "Pull up! Not too hard."

Seth lifted his pole. It bowed over the lake, its tip almost touching the water.

"Whoo Hoo!" shouted Gramps. "Now reel it in, nice and steady."

With his pulse pounding in his ears, Seth reeled with trembling fingers. He leaned back as the line pulled hard away from him. Finally, a shiny fish swam back and forth in the shallow water at his feet.

Gramps held Seth's line up with a small fish energetically flipping back and forth on the end.

"Now, that's a mighty fine rainbow trout," said Gramps, smiling "It's a bit on the small side, though, so we're going to put him back to let him grow a little more." He wet his hand and carefully took the hook out of the fish's lip. Then he held the little trout in the water for a few minutes before letting it go.

A few minutes later, Gramps' line began bouncing up and down like a loose spring. "Get the net!" he said, alternately lifting the pole and spinning the reel.

Seth looked quickly around.

"Right there! By the tackle box."

Seth found the silver-colored ring with a green net hanging from it.

"Hold it under the fish!" Gramps lifted his pole from the water. A big silver fish flipped wildly back and forth on the end of the line spraying drops of water in Seth's face as he leaned out with the net.

"Good job!" Gramps said, smiling.

By the time the sun was high in the sky, two more fat fish splashed on the stringer in the water. Seth had caught another one, but it got away before he could pull it all the way in.

Gramps cast his line out again and propped the pole up between some rocks. He leaned against the boulder and reached into a basket, pulling out two sandwiches. He tossed one to Seth.

Seth sat down cross-legged on the ground and downed the sandwich in four big bites.

While Gramps chewed in silence, Seth pulled his cell phone out of his back pocket. He eagerly turned it on. *Please!* He thought desperately. *Please let there be a signal!* He pinched his lips together when the words "No Signal" appeared on the screen. He suddenly hated the lake and fish and stupid fresh air.

Gramps finished eating and stood up, dusting crumbs off his jeans. "I think these fish will be enough for tonight," he said, reeling in his line. He and Seth gathered up the fishing gear in silence and headed back toward the truck.

As Gramps loaded the gear into the truck bed, he said. "You know, I need to go down the mountain tomorrow morning for some supplies. Why don't you come along? There might be a net in town you can use."

Seth smiled. "Thanks, Gramps."

Chapter 3

The next morning, Riley's excited barking pulled Seth out of his dreams. He had shut the door tight the night before to keep the annoying animal out.

"Breakfast," said Gramps, giving Seth's door a couple of quick knocks as he strode away down the hall.

Seth sat up and pulled his shirt away from his body. It was stiff from cleaning fish the night before. He wrinkled his nose. It stunk too. Yanking it over his head, he threw it into the corner where it slumped to the floor.

He lifted a clean Colorado Buffaloes T-Shirt out of his suitcase, yanked it over his head and stood up to open the door. When he turned the knob, Riley pushed into the room and lifted his nose into the air. The dog found the dirty shirt, picked it up in his mouth and ran down the hallway.

"Hey! Come back with that!" Seth ran down the stairs after the dog just as Gran came out of the kitchen.

"What's all the ruckus?" she asked. Riley darted behind her into the kitchen.

"Riley took my shirt." Seth pointed.

Gran opened the kitchen door. "Riley."

Nothing.

"Riley, you come here."

The dog appeared without the shirt.

"Go get it."

Riley hung his head and then reappeared with the shirt in his mouth.

"Drop it," said Gran.

The dog did as he was told. Then he sulked back into the kitchen.

Gran picked up the shirt. "Whew!" She held it out. "This needs a date with the washing machine! She eyed his jeans suspiciously. "The pants too. Come on." She waved to Seth to follow her.

Next to the kitchen was a small room with a washer and dryer.

"You know how these work?" asked Gran, pointing to the machines.

"Yes."

"Alright. You have two choices. You can either wash all your dirty clothes – including your undershorts and socks, or I will take them off and do it for you."

"She's not kidding either," said Gramps, who had walked up behind them. "She'll take them right off you."

"I'll do it myself," said Seth. His voice jumped up on the last word.

Gran nodded. "The soap's right there." She pointed. "When you're finished changing, come in the kitchen and have some breakfast."

Seth hurried back to his room and pulled on a clean pair of undershorts and Levi's. Then he ran downstairs and pushed all his clothes into the washer, added soap and turned it on.

He pressed his hair down with his hand and slid into a kitchen chair.

"Be sure to pick up some chicken wire while you're there." Gran said to Gramps as she put a jar of marmalade on the table. "The fence has come apart at that weak spot again and the hens keep getting out."

Gramps nodded. "Will do." He slathered a piece of toast with marmalade.

Seth looked down. Two bumpy lumps sat on his plate, covered with a thick white sauce.

"Its biscuits and gravy," said Gramps, scooping a big bite into his mouth. "Good stuff."

Seth carved off a small piece and gingerly pulled it off the fork with his teeth. Sausage and tender crumbs tickled his tongue. Mmmm. He shoveled the rest in his mouth while Gran and Gramps slowly ate theirs.

"More?" asked Gran when he had finished his second plate.

Seth held his middle. "No, thanks Gran." He thought he might explode if he tried to put anything else in his stomach.

"Let's get a move-on then," said Gramps, grabbing his keys off the table. He leaned over to plant a kiss on Gran's cheek. "We'll catch lunch in town, but be back in time for supper," he said.

As the truck bounced down the mountain a few minutes later, Seth pulled his cell phone out of his pocket and checked the charge. 98%. Good thing he'd plugged it in the night before. Riley leaned over to sniff the devise, leaving a trail of slobber behind.

"Geez, Riley," Seth groaned disgustedly. He wiped the phone on his pant leg. Then the dog licked Seth's ear. He closed his eyes and sighed. "How far is it into town?" he asked, scooting as far away from Riley as possible.

"A little less than an hour, give or take," said Gramps, "but we'll stop at a little gas station near here and fill up."

Seth held his phone close to his chest and held his right arm out to brace himself against the jarring of the truck.

A few minutes later, Gramps pulled up to a gas pump under a sign that said, "Gas N Go." As Gramps and Seth stepped out onto the pavement, Riley bounded out of the truck and darted into the nearby trees.

A short, thin man with a protruding Adams apple walked out of an open garage. Deep lines shot away from his eyes and patches of gray and black hairs poked out from under his Seattle Mariners baseball cap.

"Mornin' Clint," the man said, wiping his hands on a dirty rag. "You got visitors?" He squinted at Seth.

"Mornin' Ted," Gramps said as he put the hose into the gas tank. "This is my grandson, Seth." He watched the numbers on the pump roll over.

"You Bowmans like to grow them tall, don't you?" Ted remarked as he picked up a squeegee from a bucket by the pump and started washing the truck windshield.

Gramps threw his wallet to Seth. "Why don't you go in and buy twenty dollars gas and pick out a couple of sodas for us."

The smell of gasoline and oil floated around Seth as he made his way across the black top to a small store attached to the open garage. Cans of motor oil sat in neat rows on shelves behind the high windows.

A bell jingled from the top of the door as he stepped into the store. He chose two root beers from a cooler by the big window and put them on the counter by the cash register.

"Be right with you," yelled a deep voice from the garage.

After some grunting and scraping, a big man appeared in the side doorway. He reminded Seth of the linebackers he had seen playing football on TV. He was wearing gray coveralls with a patch on his pocket that said "Cal" and was completely bald.

What we got here?" Cal asked as he stepped behind the counter. A cigarette hung out of one corner of his mouth and tattoos covered his arms.

"Twenty gallons of gas and these sodas," Seth said, trying not to stare.

As the man rang up the gas and pop, Seth looked out the window to see Gramps and Ted leaning over the truck hood talking. Gramps was frowning and shaking his head.

"Clint Bowman is your Grandpa?" Cal asked as he handed the change to Seth.

"Yes," said Seth as he picked up the cans of root beer.

Seth felt Cal's eyes on his back as he stepped out the door.

Walking back to the truck, he heard Ted say, "Two more dogs disappeared last week."

"We're going to have to find out where the next fight is and catch them in the act. It's the only way," said Gramps. "Riley! Come on!"

Gramps opened the door and Riley burst out of the trees and jumped up onto the seat. Seth climbed in the passenger side and nudged the dog over with his elbow.

"It's that dog fighting bunch," Gramps said as he turned the key and jerked the truck into first gear." "Looks like they're at it again. Pets are missing from people's yards. Small animals turning up dead…"

"But didn't they throw the fighters in jail two years ago when you found Riley?"

"Well, we think we know who is responsible, but there was never enough evidence for the sheriff to make any arrests."

Seth let out a low whistle.

"The problem is that they're always moving around. One night, they set up in an abandoned warehouse, another in someone's barn." He shifted gears. "Constantly changing the time and location makes it hard to expose their operation."

After another half hour of winding roads, Gramps pulled into a parking spot in front of a store with the words "Harry's Hardware and Supply" painted in bright green letters on the front.

"Why don't you run over to the café and see if they have net you can use," said Gramps, nodding toward a low building on the other side of the street with cars and trucks hunched around it.

Seth jumped out of the truck and hurried across the street. Walking under a neon sign that read, "The Cat's Meow," he pulled open a glass door and stepped inside.

A woman with a light blue uniform and a name tag that said "Inez" looked up from wiping a table. "Be right with you," she said.

Seth felt the stares of the other diners in the place as the clinking of dishes surrounded him. He studied his shoes and tapped the sides of his legs.

"How many?" said Inez, standing in front of him with a handful of plastic menus. Her straw-colored hair was piled neatly on the top of her head.

"Um. Two."

She smiled and led him to a booth near the back window.

He slid onto the red vinyl and watched the door for Gramps.

"What can I get you?" Inez asked. She held a pencil over a pad of paper.

"I'm waiting for my Grandpa," he said. "Do you have internet here?"

"No. We don't. Sorry." She lowered the pencil and walked away.

Seth wanted to throw his phone across the room. He propped his face up with his left hand and followed the pattern of the tablecloth with his eyes. A few minutes later, he felt the table jiggle as Gramps sat down across from him, but he didn't look up.

"I guess they don't have any net here," Gramps said.

Seth tried to answer but his throat was closed so he just gave a short shake of his head.

Inez walked up to the table. "Hi Clint! I didn't know you had such a handsome visitor," she smiled at Seth.

"This is my Grandson, Seth. Looks just like his dad," Gramps smiled. "Say, you wouldn't know anywhere in town they might have some phone net do you?"

Her eyes went to the phone in Seth's hand. "You might have to go into Kalispell for internet," she said. Then, "What'll you have?" she held up her pad.

"Coffee please. Black. You want anything?" he asked Seth. "They have excellent burgers and fries here."

Seth shook his head again.

"How about you make us a couple of cheeseburgers and a big batch of fries and we'll take them with us," said Gramps.

"Coming right up," she said, walking away.

"Clint Bowman," said a voice from the booth behind Seth. A man stood up and stepped over to their table. He reminded Seth of Mr. Smee from the movie "Hook." He was short and round with a few strands of steel gray hair combed over a shiny head. A brass belt buckle the size of Seth's hand with the letters SJ carved in it pressed into his belly. His bulging nose was the size and color of a plum.

"You know, my dog, Prissy is missing from my yard?" the man said, leaning on the table with his eyes on Gramps. "And that *mutt*," he pointed at Riley, who was sitting outside in front of the glass door staring at them, "is responsible."

"How do you mean, responsible?" asked Gramps.

"The last time you brought that mangy beast down here, I caught him digging under the fence in my backyard. I chased him off, but now my best breeder is missing. She must have escaped from the hole *he* dug. So, what I want from you is to know what you are going to do about it?"

"Look, Stan, you could just put out some missing dog posters. I'm sure she'll show up."

Stan's face flushed red and he clenched his fists. "She's a papered Staffordshire! If she goes into heat before I get her back, it'll be too late. I need some pure-bred puppies to sell by the end of the summer. I have buyers waiting!" Now his voice had taken on a whiny tone.

"So, you want me to buy you another puppy machine to replace her?"

"It was your dog that did the damage." Stan straightened up with a satisfied look.

Inez returned with a cup of coffee and placed it in front of Gramps. "Stan, you harassing my customers?" she asked.

Stan pinched his lips together in a thin line, took a ten-dollar bill out of his wallet and threw it on his table.

"I'll be by your place to discuss this further," he growled. He gave Gramps a hard look, then stalked away.

Chapter 4

"Hand me those pliers," Gramps said, pointing to an open tool box. Seth rummaged through the tools.

Gramps squatted by the chicken coop fence and pulled the two sides together with his left hand while he held out his right hand toward Seth. Riley lay in the shade next to him noisily chewing last night's ham bone.

"These ones?" Seth held up a pair of needle-nose pliers.

"No. Those combination ones – with the blue handles."

Seth handed them over.

While Gramps wrestled with the chicken wire, he said, "Seth, I'm sorry about your phone game. Kalispell is another two hours down the mountain, so we'll have to plan an overnighter."

"I don't feel like playing anyway," Seth lied. He knew his mom would kill him if she found out he had made Gramps drive that far just so he could play *Demon Quest*. Besides, he wasn't sure he could take being jostled in the pickup truck for three hours straight. His joints still ached from the trip into town.

"You know," Gramps looked at Seth out of the side of his eyes, "There are some games you can play without a phone or a net."

Right, Seth thought. *Go Fish.*

"Alright, that should about do it," Gramps said as he stood and brushed the dirt off his jeans. "Let's see you ladies get through THAT." He grabbed the toolbox while Seth lifted the extra wire and followed him into the garage.

Looking around in the half light, Seth saw rows of jars filled with screws and nails on a bench covered with wood scraps. A couple of bikes with flat tires sat next to a rusty lawn mower. Gramps followed Seth's eyes. He walked over and pulled one of the bikes away from the wall. The frame was bent, and the seat torn.

"Your dad used to ride these bikes all over the mountain," he said. "He wrecked this one here. That's why it's all bent out of shape. This other one is newer, but the chain is broke, and the gears are out of whack." He reached down and examined the tires. "Let's pump 'em up and see how many holes they have."

They were still working on the bikes by the time Gran opened the back door and called out that supper was ready. As Seth and Gramps hurried to the house, Gran stood in the doorway with her right hand on her hip and her left hand pointing to the water spigot at the side of the house. Eyeing each other like guilty three-year-olds, they moved to the spigot and rinsed their hands and faces.

After a quick inspection, a short nod from Gran allowed them into the kitchen. Seth took a deep breath. Mmmm. Apple pie. He was beginning to understand why Gramps was as round as he was.

When Seth was so full of roast beef and mashed potatoes, he could hardly move, Gramps said, "Hey, let's make some ice-cream to go with that pie." He jumped up and started rummaging in the cupboards. "Lou, where is that ice cream maker?"

"I think we put it up in the attic," answered Gran as she started taking dishes off the table.

"Uh, can I help load the dishwasher?" Seth asked.

Gran laughed. "The only dishwasher around here is standing right there." She pointed to Gramps.

Gramps smiled, threw a dishtowel to Seth, and started filling the sink with hot water.

"You know, there's a great swimming hole on the other side of the lake. You can't drive there, but I can show you the trail to follow.

Seth's eyes went to the window.

"Know how to swim?" Gramps asked, handing him a plate.

Seth nodded and pushed the towel around the plate. But he wasn't sure he wanted to swim someplace where he couldn't see the bottom. Would a fish bite his toe?

Once the dishes were clean and put away, Gramps led Seth past the bedrooms to a narrow flight of stairs. They went up single file to a wooden door at the top.

"It's been a while since we've been up here," Gramps said, opening the door to a loud creak. A musty smell flowed out of the attic as he pushed it open. Reaching above his head, Gramps pulled on a string and a bare bulb clicked on. Seth squinted through the feeble light at lumps of dusty shapes.

"It must be around here somewhere," Gramps said as he stepped around an old chest.

Riley pushed by Seth's leg, his toenails clicking on the wood floor and he nosed through the boxes and caused dust to float through the air.

Seth sneezed. "Is it big?" he asked.

"It looks like a bucket with a handle. About like this." Gramps gestured with his hands. He opened a box and looked inside.

Seth sat on a stack of newspapers and looked around. He spotted a board leaning against the wall and lifted it from the floor. Blowing off the dust, he coughed and waved his hand in front of his nose. Attached to the board was a gold painted flyswatter with a metal plate on the bottom. He peered at the wording. "Arrive and Fly Award?" he asked, reading the plate aloud.

Gramps turned, looked at the plaque then turned back to open another box. "When I was in the service, I was called up as a medic at DaNang Air Base during the Viet Nam war." He pulled a sweater out of the box and held it up. It was green with a large yellow "O" on the front. "Will you look at that." He held it in front of him. "My letterman's sweater. The Oregon Ducks." He smiled at Seth. "Don't suppose it would fit me anymore." He dropped it back in the box.

"Anyway," he went on, digging, "One of our jobs was to meet the helicopters bringing in the casualties. Lots of times these big biting flies would land on the wounded men. Some of them didn't even have arms to shoo them away." He pointed to the flyswatter. "So, I started carrying that in my back pocket to keep the flies off."

"Wow," said Seth softly.

"My buddies hid it from me near the end of my tour of duty. Painted it gold and mounted it. They awarded it to me on my last day."

Gramps lifted a guitar case and put it on a small table in the corner.

"Cool!" said Seth. He opened the case and studied the guitar inside. "Do you play?"

"Your Gran does. She used to be pretty good, too. Played at the county fair five years in a row." He leaned against the wall. "That was where I first saw her. I was on leave from the Air Force, just getting ready to head back to the base." He stared above Seth's head as if he was seeing it all again. "She was up there on stage with that curly red hair playing and singing – had the whole crowd clapping and singing along." He smiled. "For me, it was love at first sight. Not so much for her. She was having a lot of fun dating a couple of locals and didn't see much of a future with a skinny kid like me."

Seth looked at Gramps' round belly. He had a hard time imagining him as skinny.

"I spent every spare minute I had coming back to see her and chasing away the competition." He pulled out another box from behind a chair. "I guess she was finally won over by my rascally good looks." His eyebrows bobbed up and down. Seth smiled.

Seth took the guitar out of the worn case and brushed his thumb over the strings. It sounded like a cat being murdered.

"Probably hasn't been tuned in twenty years," Gramps said, bending over the box. "Ah. Here it is!" He blew dust off a bucket. Turning toward the attic door, he nodded at the guitar. "Why don't you bring that along too. Maybe Gran will play us one of her old songs."

As Gramps and Seth reached the kitchen, Gran was coming in the kitchen door with an apron full of eggs.

"Look what else we found," Gramps said, holding up the guitar.

Gran eyed the guitar and shook her head. "It's been quite a while." She moved to the sink. "Let me clean these eggs first, and then maybe we'll see what your old Gran can pull out of her memory banks." She smiled at Seth.

Seth had never seen so many shades and sizes of eggs. Some were brown, and some were even light green! And he'd never heard of eggs that needed cleaning. He stared at the blobs of sticky white goo and bits of straw on them.

"I'll take a couple of those," Gramps said as he took two clean eggs from the towel by the sink. "Now, let's see, we need some cream." He opened the fridge and put his head in. "Seth, grab the canister of sugar in that cupboard there," he pointed as he pulled a carton out and put it on the countertop.

Once everything was loaded into the ice-cream maker, Gran showed Seth how to turn the handle sticking out of the side. He sat down at the table and cranked it around and around while Gran sat down and pulled the guitar onto her lap. After picking at the strings and twisting the pegs, she started singing in a strong, sweet voice. If she was out of practice, Seth sure couldn't tell it. She sang a silly song about sweet violets with Gramps joining in on the chorus.

Seth's arm began to ache as it went round and round. Then, just when he thought his grandparents had forgotten all about him, Gramps announced that the ice-cream was ready to be checked. He lifted the lid and poked a spoon into the soft cream and licked it. "Mmm. What do you think Lou?"

Gran took out a clean spoon and took a small taste. "Still a little soft."

Seth sighed and started turning the crank again. No ice-cream was worth this, he thought. He cranked through two more songs before Gran declared the ice-cream ready.

She loaded a scoop on top of a big piece of pie for Seth and made two more plates for Gramps and herself. The sweet frozen cream melted on Seth's tongue. He took another big spoonful. Then another. Before long the plate was empty, and he was scraping up the drips at the bottom.

"I think a growing boy needs another helping," said Gran, scooping more into his plate with a smile. She put her empty plate on the floor where Riley's dog tags clinked against it as he licked it with gusto.

As Seth was finishing up his third helping, Gramps turned to him and said, "You feel up to playing a game for only the toughest competitors?"

"Ok," said Seth doubtfully.

Riley followed Gramps and Seth into the living room and curled up by the fireplace as Gramps arranged the chairs on opposite sides of a small table. Opening a drawer, he pulled out a red and black checkered board and dumped round wooden disks onto it.

"Checkers!" said Seth. "I learned to play checkers when I was eight years old!"

"Did you? Then this will be easy for you."

"Clint..." said Gran, as she sat on the edge of the couch with her guitar.

"He knows how to play, Lou. He said so."

Gramps spread the checkers over the board and turned the black side toward Seth.

"You go first."

Ten minutes later, all Seth's checkers lay in a pile beside the board.

Gramps set up the game again. "You can't win by hugging the sides. You might have to sacrifice one of your men so another can be kinged."

This time it took twenty minutes for Gramps to capture all Seth's checkers.

As Gramps spread out the checkers again, he said, "Now, this time, try to think two or three moves ahead. Don't just randomly move to what looks like a temporary safe spot. Try to bait me into doing what you want."

An hour later, Seth and Gramps hovered over the last three kings on the board.

Seth sighed and sat back. "You got me again, Gramps."

"Ah, but you put up quite a good fight that time!"

That night Seth stared at the ceiling with his arms folded under his head. He was glad Gramps didn't let him win. It showed that he thought Seth was capable of winning on his own. And the ice-cream had been pretty good too.

Chapter 5

It took Gramps and Seth a week to combine two broken bicycles into one.

"Ok," Gramps said at last. "Try that out."

Seth swung his leg over the bar and lifted himself onto the seat. Riley barked his approval as Seth rode in a circle in front of the garage.

"Hold on," said Gramps reaching out for the bike.

Seth stopped and Gramps raised the seat a little higher and tightened it. Then he stepped back and said, "Alright, see how that feels."

The wind twisted Seth's hair in wild loops above his head as he flew out of the yard. He turned toward the lake road and pushed the pedals in rapid circles. Enjoying the feel of the sun warming his back, he swerved to avoid a striped chipmunk that dashed in front of him. Riley happily barked and chased the small animal into the plants and bushes at the side of the road.

As his breath came in bigger gulps, Seth wondered if there might be cell phone reception farther up the mountain. He peddled faster past giant evergreens reaching for the sky. As the road narrowed, branches snatched at his shirt and slapped his legs. He pinched the hand breaks, slowing.

Suddenly the road gave out all together in front of an old log small cabin. He skidded to a stop.

"Hello?" he called.

Only the wind blowing through the trees answered. Black window holes watched Seth as he leaned the bicycle against a tree.

He tested each of the weathered steps in front of the craggy building with his foot before adding his whole weight. Then he slowly went up the planks. They were creaky, but solid. He shielded his eyes with his hands and looked through the windows.

Seth tried the front door. It swung open easily. Bales of straw formed a square in the middle of the floor, but there was no furniture in sight.

Why would anyone put hay inside their house? He wondered.

A muffled bark followed by a low whine interrupted his thoughts.

"Riley?"

He turned and jumped off the porch, stopping at the bottom to listen. The whimpering came again from somewhere to his left. He moved toward the sound, crunching twigs and leaves under his feet. At an opening in the bushes, he saw Riley standing by – what was it? A deer? No. The animal didn't look anything like the pictures of deer he had seen in school; and the color was too light. Riley whimpered as he sniffed the caramel-colored animal that lay curled up under a bush. As Seth stepped closer, he saw the short broad head of a dog.

"Where did you come from?" he asked, as he squatted next to Riley. Was it dead? He touched the coarse fur with a finger. The head rose and looked at Seth through glazed eyes. Then it dropped again.

Seth's stomach rose into his throat. "Stay here, Riley," he said as he turned and ran through the trees. Reaching the bike, he swung a shaky leg over it.

His lungs burned as he peddled wildly down the road. He began yelling for Gramps as soon as the house came into view. By the time he jumped off the bike, Gramps was out on the porch with his eyebrows knit together.

"A dog," Seth said breathlessly, pointing down the road. "There's a hurt dog in a clearing."

Gramps' eyebrows rose to his hairline. He disappeared into the house and came out with a blanket and his keys.

Seth wheeled the bike into the garage and opened the right truck door. The truck roared to life as Seth jumped onto the front seat.

"How far?" Gramps asked.

Seth hesitated. "At the end of the road. There's an old cabin."

"Sounds like the old Ferguson place." Gramps shifted gears. "And you left Riley there?"

"Yes."

"Good."

When they reached cabin, Gramps slammed the truck into park and turned off the key. He jumped out of the truck as Seth grabbed the blanket and slid onto the ground.

"Riley!" called Gramps.

A muffled bark came from the bushes.

"That way!" said Seth, pointing.

They crashed through the trees and found Riley and the dog just as Seth had left them.

Gramps squatted by the dog and put his hand on its side. It didn't move. "I think it's Stan Juke's dog, Prissy," he said softly. "She was alive when you found her?"

Tears pricked Seth's eyelids. "She lifted her head when I touched her."

Gramps moved expert hands along her legs and back. "Nothing seems broken." He examined her neck and belly. "I don't see any lacerations." He lowered his head onto her side. "I think I hear a heartbeat – barely." He reached his hand toward Seth. "Let's get her back to the house."

Seth handed him the blanket and together they slid it under Prissy and lifted her from the ground. Back at the truck, Seth climbed onto the front seat and Gramps laid Prissy across his lap. Then he and Riley squeezed in the driver's side.

Back at the house, Gran made the dog a bed in front of the stove in the kitchen. "She'll be warmer in here," she said, turning the oven on low.

Seth sat on the floor and gently petted Prissy's head as Gramps and Gran left the room. He listened to their disjointed voices coming through the door.

"Do you think…?"

"I don't know…in bad shape."

Chapter 6

The next morning Seth woke up on the kitchen floor with two dark brown eyes staring back at him. Sometime during the night, someone had put a pillow under his head and covered him with the quilt from his bed. Prissy licked up the last of some milk in a bowl in front of her.

"She's still weak, but I think she's going to make it," said Gramps, buttoning his shirt as he came into the kitchen. "She just needed something to eat." Riley followed him into the kitchen and sniffed Prissy. Then he went to his dish and gobbled up his dog food.

Seth slowly reached out a hand and let Prissy smell him. She sniffed the fingers and then laid her head on her front paws, watching him warily.

"Give her some space and don't make any sudden movements," said Gramps, pulling out a chair. "We don't know what she's been through. She might not trust humans."

Gran put a plate of scrambled eggs and bacon in front of Gramps. "Come and eat," she said to Seth, patting the table, "then you can see if she is strong enough to go outside."

Seth jumped up and threw himself into the chair, squeezed his eyes shut as Gramps pronounced a blessing, and then shoveled breakfast into his mouth. When his plate was empty, he slid down to the floor and sat cross-legged next to Prissy.

The dog scooted over to Seth and licked a bit of egg off his shirt. Then she looked at him expectantly.

"You hungry, girl?" Seth asked. "She's hungry Gran."

"All right," said Gran. "Give her a little of this. Not too much all at once." She handed Seth a small bowl of scrambled eggs.

As soon as Seth put the bowl in front of her, Prissy eagerly pushed her nose into the bowl and swallowed the food. When the eggs were gone, she eyed Seth, licking her lips.

"That's probably enough for now," said Gramps. "She's awfully thin and too much might make her sick."

The dog laid her head in Seth's lap and sighed. He slowly reached out a hand and ran it over the rows of ribs lining her side.

Gran handed Seth a bowl of water and he offered it to Prissy. She lapped up a few mouthfuls, then rose on shaky legs.

"Let's see if she needs to go outside," said Gran. She opened the kitchen door.

"Come on, girl, come on," said Seth as he stood and went to the door. Prissy took a couple of wobbly steps toward him.

"Good girl!" he said. "You can do it." He patted his thighs.

Slowly, the dog made her way outside where she squatted to relieve herself. Then she walked over to a tree, lay down and closed her eyes.

The rest of the morning, Seth stayed by her side, softly rubbing her head and talking to her in a soothing voice. Riley came out and nudged the muffin brown dog with his nose, then lay down next to her. Around noon, Gran brought a sandwich out and handed it to Seth.

"Thanks Gran," said Seth, taking a huge bite. The tang of mayonnaise and turkey filled his mouth.

Both dogs lifted their heads and stared at the sandwich with eager eyes. Seth tore off a corner of turkey meat and held it out for Prissy. She delicately took the meat from his hand and scarfed it down. Riley immediately sat up and looked at Seth with laser eyes.

"All right," said Seth, tearing off a piece and tossing it to the scruffy dog.

After he had eaten about half the sandwich, with the dogs eating the other half, Seth stood and stretched. Looking toward the kitchen door, he said, "I wonder if there is any leftover pie."

Hurrying to the door, he opened it and stepped inside. Gran looked up from wiping off the table. "That was fast," she said, looking past him through the open door. "How much of that sandwich did the dogs talk you out of?"

Seth turned to see Riley and Prissy right behind him and grinned. "About half," he admitted.

Gran smiled. "Well, she is looking much better, I must say," she said, her twinkling eyes watching Prissy over his shoulder. She made Seth another sandwich and handed it to him. Then, she pulled an old bowl out of the cupboard and filled it half full of dog food. "Here you go, Prissy," she said putting the dish on the floor.

"You already had your breakfast," she said to Riley. He slunk to the floor and put his head on his paws.

Seth made short work of the sandwich and wiped his mouth with his sleeve.

"I don't suppose you would be interested in some pie now?" Gran asked.

"I sure would!"

Gran dished up some of the desert and put the plate and a fork in front of him.

"Thanks Gran!" He said, diving in with gusto.

She smiled indulgently. "Glad you like it." She filled a glass of milk and put it in front of him.

"Did somebody say pie?" asked Gramps coming into the kitchen. He rubbed his eyes and scratched his head.

"For those who come for lunch when I call them, yes," said Gran.

"Well, I was working on something and didn't hear you," said Gramps.

"You were working on your snoring repertoire?" she asked, a smirk playing at the corners of her mouth. She put a sandwich and a piece of pie in front of him.

"Well, she's looking perky this afternoon," Gramps nodded at Prissy as she finished the last of the dog food. "We'll give her a couple more days to recover, then we'll have to go down the mountain and have a talk with Stan."

Seth's throat closed. "But if she's been neglected…" he began.

"We need to find out for sure what's going on." Gramps took a bite. "If Stan finds out she's up here, he might come after her and legally we couldn't stop him."

Chapter 7

The moon showed brightly through Seth's window as he pulled the covers up under his chin that night. Just as he was drifting off, he heard a soft clicking downstairs. He sat up. There it was again. *Click click, scratch, click.* Was Gramps putting away the checkers or Gran putting the chairs back in the kitchen?

Wearing only his t-shirt and underwear, he crept out into the dark hallway and listened.

The moonlight shown out of his room and down the dark stairway. Two shiny eyes stared back at him. Prissy was slowly making her way up the stairs on shaky legs. Seth inched down to where the skinny dog was struggling and pushed her up the final stairs from behind.

Seth guided her into his room and quietly clicked the door shut behind them. He sat on his bed and she sat by his leg looking reverently up into his face. He scratched her head, whispering, "You're such a pretty dog."

Prissy's tail thumped against the floor.

"Want to come up here?" Seth patted the bed next to him. The dog reached up with her two front paws and lowered her head, pushing with wobbly back legs. Seth helped her onto the bed like a sailor helping a drowning swimmer into a lifeboat. Once on the bed, she flipped over and showed a soft underbelly.

"You like your tummy rubbed?" Seth whispered. He felt the silky-smooth fur of her stomach.

The next morning, Seth woke in a tangle of sheets half off the bed with his right hand dragging on the floor. He twisted around to see Prissy stretched out in the middle of the bed with her head on his pillow. She opened an eye and shut it again, sighing.

There was a tap on his door, followed by Gran's voice saying, "Breakfast in twenty minutes. You have time for a quick shower."

Seth sat up and sniffed his arm pit. He guessed a shower wouldn't hurt. After pulling on his jeans, he opened his door to be nearly knocked down by Riley who ran into the room barking excitedly.

Prissy lifted her head and thumped the bed with her tail.

Gramps poked his head in and said, "Well. She made it clear up here by herself, did she?"

"Mostly," admitted Seth.

"And she's made herself at home, I see."

Seth snickered. "Yeah."

"Alright, bring her down after you get cleaned up and we'll see how her appetite is this morning." He patted his leg. "Come on, Riley."

Riley ran out of the room and thumped down the stairs after Gramps.

Prissy crawled off the bed and followed Seth down the hall to the tiny bathroom. When he shut the door and turned on the tap, she started whining outside the door.

"There's no room in here!" he yelled through the door as he pulled off his shirt.

The dog began to howl.

Finally, he opened the door and looked out. Prissy pushed her nose through the opening.

"Fine," he said, rolling his eyes. He stood behind the door and let her into the small space. Stepping over her, he climbed into the tub and pulled the curtain closed. As he turned on the water and let the warm spray wash over his back, he saw a caramel snout poking under the shower curtain.

By the time Seth finished his shower, the clothes he had left on the bathroom floor were sopping wet, and Prissy was soaked as well. He put his shirt and pants on anyway and went down to breakfast with the dripping dog right behind him.

Gran's eyebrows went up at the sight of their watery footprints on the kitchen tile.

Gramps said, "Well, I prefer to wash my body and my clothes separately, but I guess that's one way to save some time." He smiled and took a bite of toast.

"Whew!" said Gran, "I thought I smelled something! Go ahead and have something to eat, and then take her outside and finish the job with soap." She pointed at Prissy.

After breakfast, Prissy eyed Seth dejectedly as he sponged her down with soap and dumped buckets of water from the outside spigot over her.

"Don't give me that look," he said. "You brought this on yourself – hey!" Seth held an arm over his face as she shook herself vigorously, flinging droplets of water all over him and the side of the house. His half dry clothes were now drenched again. Prissy trotted around the yard sniffing every bush and tree like a four-legged detective. When she reached the chicken coop, her ears went up and her head tipped to the side. The chickens ignored the dog and went about their business of scratching and pecking at the ground behind the wire fence.

"Woof!" Prissy barked, wagging her tail.

The chickens stretched out their wings and dashed around the enclosure in circles, clucking loudly.

"No!" said Seth. "Leave those chickens alone."

Prissy looked up at Seth with wide eyes.

"That's right," said Seth. "They don't want to play."

He took a step backwards. "COME, Prissy, COME." He patted his thighs.

She sat down and stared at him.

"No. COME. Like this." He reached out and gently pulled on her collar.

Prissy stepped cautiously forward.

"Good girl!" He stepped farther back and patted his legs.

"Come Prissy!"

She bolted toward him and jumped up, knocking him back with her paws.

"Whoa! Ok ok. Good dog," Seth laughed.

He held his hand up, palm forward. "Stay." He turned and took a step. The dog followed immediately, wagging her tail happily.

"No." Sigh. "Prissy. STAY HERE." He inched backwards in slow motion with his hand out in front of him. Prissy sat and tipped her head to the side.

He walked to the other side of the yard.

"Co…!"

Before Seth could finish, Prissy burst toward him and pushed him down onto the ground.

He dissolved into laughter as she happily licked his face.

"You're a smart dog, yes you are," said Seth, smiling and scratching her head.

Prissy's ears pricked up and she darted back around the side of the house, her barking echoing through the yard.

"I said to leave those chickens alone!" Seth groaned as he stood up and brushed himself off. He stomped around the corner in time to see Prissy chasing a small reddish-brown animal into the trees.

Gran came out of the house with a broom in her hand. "What's all the commotion?"

Riley darted out of the house and followed Prissy into the woods.

"Prissy went after some animal with red fur and a bushy tail."

"That trouble-making fox is back." Gran said to the open doorway behind her. Then she asked Seth, "Which way did they go?"

He pointed.

She raised the broom and charged after them.

Gramps came out onto the step and put his hands into his pockets. "That critter's not going to be happy if the dogs catch up with it. But it'll be worse for the fox if Gran gets to it first."

Chapter 8

"King me!" Seth pushed a checker to a square on the opposite side of the board.

"Well, that was just plain sneaky," said Gramps.

"I learned from the best," Seth smiled.

A flash of lighting splashed through the room followed by the rumble of thunder. An afternoon storm had blown in, and Gran had started a fire to chase away the chilly air. She looked up from strumming her guitar and shook her head at Riley, who lay on the floor by Gramps snoring loudly.

Prissy pressed herself against Seth's leg, quivering.

"It's just noise," Seth said, petting her head. "It'll be OK." It was hard to believe that the same dog that bravely chased away a fox a few days before was now terrified of a little storm.

At that moment, the room went abruptly dark.

"Not again," said Gramps' voice.

The dying embers in the fireplace gave a soft glow to the room and shadows sprang up on the walls. Gran stood and made her way to a cabinet next to the kitchen door. A door clicked open, and she shuffled around. Then she lifted something out and flicked it on. A beam of light shone on the wall.

"Here you go," she said, handing Seth the flashlight. "We'll use this candle." She scratched a match to life and touched it to the wick.

"I bet another tree limb fell on one of the power lines," said Gramps. He stood and stretched. "I doubt they'll have it fixed before morning."

"Might as well go on up to bed early," said Gran.

"That's what I was thinking," said Gramps, stretching. "We best make an early night of it."

Up in his room, Seth flopped onto the bed and shined the flashlight around the room. It was too early to go to sleep. As the beam flashed on the wall, Prissy jumped at it and tried to bite the circle of light. Seth snickered. He shone the beam onto the floor and watched Prissy pounce on it again.

She looked up in confusion when the light escaped from under her and floated around her in a circle. Seth laughed out loud when she chased it to the wall and snapped at the patch of light with her teeth. He moved the beam higher and higher, watching her leap and lunge at it until he was weak with laughter.

At last, he scooted off the bed and dropped onto the floor next to her.

"See? It's just a light," he said, letting her sniff the flashlight as he rubbed her behind the ears.

His eyes moved to the shelf in the open closet. He shone the flashlight on the row of books. *Treasure Island*, he murmured. Sounded familiar. Didn't they make a movie of that one? He read, *Swiss Family Robinson* on the next spine. They'd read that one in school. He reached up and took the one on the end and read the cover. *The Hatchet*. The picture on the front showed a wolf howling. He turned it around and shined the flashlight on the back.

Thirteen-year-old Brian Robeson is on his way to visit his father when the single-engine plane in which he is flying crashes. Suddenly, Brian finds himself alone the Canadian wilderness with nothing but a tattered windbreaker and the hatchet his mother gave him as a present…"

He lay down on the bed and opened the book. Shining the flashlight on it, he read a page. Prissy jumped onto the bed and lay her head on his chest. He continued turning pages far into the night.

Chapter 9

Seth braced himself against the door of the truck as he and Gramps bounced down the mountain. Riley had stared accusingly at them as Gran held his collar and they drove away without him, but Gramps had said it was best to deal with just one dog this trip. Seth was just happy not to sit next to a slobber factory for once.

He wrapped his left arm around Prissy's warm body. As they drove by The Cat's Meow Café, Seth pictured Stan Juke's scowling face. His stomach twisted when he thought of leaving Prissy with the angry man.

Maybe Stan would let Seth buy her. He had seventy-five dollars in a shoebox under his bed at home that he had been saving up for a new smart phone. He could ask his mom to bring it with her when she came to pick him up at the end of the summer.

They pulled up to a one-story brown stucco rambler with dry yellow grass in front surrounded by a chain link fence. A wobbly mailbox with the name "Juke" on it leaned drunkenly next to the road. In the driveway, a shiny new-looking white pickup truck sat next to the shabby building.

Prissy let out a soft whimper.

"You want to wait here with the dog?" asked Gramps.

Seth swallowed and shook his head. He would need to face the man to negotiate a price for Prissy.

Gramps lifted the gate latch and they stepped onto a cracked sidewalk. Prissy trailed behind with her tail between her legs. They stepped up to the front door. It was open, but the screen door was shut.

Gramps lifted a big fist and pounded on the screen frame. "Stan," he yelled.

Rowdy barking came from behind the house.

"Stan, its Clint. We found your dog, Prissy."

There was more feverish barking.

He put his hand on his hips and looked around. "His truck is here. He must be here somewhere."

Seth followed Gramps around the side of the house where aging wood planks rose from the ground like a row of crooked teeth. Gramps put his hands on the top of the fence and looked over. Seth joined him.

In the center of the yard, a large pit-bull on a short heavy chain snarled and snapped at a tabby cat being held by the scruff of the neck in Stan Juke's hand. The man laughed each time the dog lunged and was jerked backwards at the end of the chain, just short of the terrified cat. Dozens of other dogs and puppies barked frantically from cages and chains around the yard. Empty dog dishes lay strewn around the yard next to piles of dog poop.

Icy fingers crawled up Seth's pine as Juke's eyes lifted to the fence and narrowed.

"What are you doing on my property!" he shouted. He threw the cat down and it ran out of sight in a blur. Stan stomped over toward the gate. Flinging it open, he stepped through and slammed it shut.

"Well, I see you brought back the dog you stole," he said, folding his arms.

"Seth, take Prissy and go wait in the truck," Gramps said quietly.

"Come here, Prissy," Stan ordered, pointing to the ground beside him.

The dog pressed herself into Seth's side and whined.

"Seth," said Gramps without taking his eyes off Stan.

Seth took a step to the side, then turned and ran back to the truck with Prissy on his heels. His heart pounded as he tore open the door and followed the dog onto the front seat, slamming the door behind them.

Rolling the window down, he listened to the angry voices.

"I'm calling the sheriff!" yelled Stan.

"Please do!" said Gramps. "I'm sure he'll be interested to know you're running a puppy mill."

After a few more minutes of shouting, Gramps came toward the truck shaking his head. With his jaw working, he swung open the door and slid onto the seat.

"You can't come on a man's property without his permission!" shouted Stan following him around the side of the house.

Gramps turned the key and slammed the truck into reverse. He pulled away from the house in a spray of gravel.

As they drove away, Seth turned to see Stan standing in the driveway punching the air and shouting.

They drove into town and pulled up in front of a white stone building with towering columns holding up the roof.

"Bring Prissy along," Gramps said as they stepped out of the truck.

53

Seth looked around nervously, as he jumped down from the passenger seat, half expecting Stan Juke to drive up and chase them.

"Come, Prissy," he said. She quickly followed.

Her nails clicked on the highly polished floor tiles in the building as they made their way down a long hallway. Gramps opened a glass door with the words "County Sheriff" stenciled above a government symbol.

"Can I help you?" asked a smiling woman with jet black hair and bright red lipstick. Her eyes widened at the site of Prissy next to Seth.

"We need to see the Sheriff," said Gramps.

A man with ebony skin and a silver badge on his left shirt pocket appeared. He was a head shorter than Seth but stood ramrod straight with bulging muscles straining at the shoulders of his tan uniform. Strands of gray blended with his short, dark curly hair.

"Clint Bowman! I thought I heard your voice," he said, "Come on back." He waved Gramps and Seth into his office.

They sat in stiff chairs in front of a desk with a name plate that said, "Sheriff Gerald Keller" on it. Prissy hid under Seth's legs.

"So, what's with the dog?" the Sheriff asked as he pulled a leather office chair up behind a massive wood desk.

"She's evidence, Jerry," Gramps answered.

"Alright," said the sheriff. He leaned back with his fingers pressed together. "What's the story?"

Gramps filled him in on Prissy and what they had seen at Stan Juke's place. The sheriff came around the desk and looked at the thin quivering dog. He rubbed his hand gently over her protruding ribs.

"Looks like we can hold him for animal cruelty and running a puppy mill," mused the Sheriff as he straitened and leaned against the desk. "But I don't want to arrest him yet. He may be involved in that dog fighting ring, and we've been hoping he'll lead us to the perpetrators."

At that moment angry voices came from the other side of the door.

"I'm sorry, Sir, he is busy right now!" Tina said. "You can't go in there!"

Stan Juke burst into the sheriff's office.

"Sheriff, I want you to arrest this man for trespassing and theft!" He pointed at Gramps.

Tina glared at him.

"I've got it, Tina, thanks," said the sheriff.

Tina whirled on her heel and stormed out.

"Stan, keep your shirt on and wait your turn."

"But he stole a very valuable animal from my place," Stan sputtered. "She's worth at least $2,000. And today he and this *kid*," he pointed at Seth, "were back over there to steal more of my dogs!"

Seth's face flushed hot, and his mouth sprang open.

"Stan, if you don't keep quiet, I'm going to throw you in jail right now for obstruction of justice!"

Stan's face darkened and he opened and closed his mouth silently like a fish out of water.

Sheriff Keller walked behind his desk, sat down, and picked up a pen.

"Now, there have been some very serious allegations made here today." He tapped the pen and looked back and forth between the men. "We are going to have to open an investigation into this matter." He pulled out a form from one of the desk drawers and started filling it out. "In the meantime, I'm going to award temporary custody of this fine animal," he smiled down at Prissy, "To – Seth Bowman, is it?"

"What!" exploded Stan.

"Or we could make it permanent, Stan, if you prefer."

Stan made a choking sound. Then he turned and stomped away.

Chapter 10

"Let's walk down to the vet and get Prissy checked out before we head back," Gramps said, as he and Seth stepped onto the sidewalk in front of the courthouse.

Seth kept a worried eye out for Stan Juke as they turned right and crossed the street.

"I expect Stan is back at his place trying to hide evidence," said Gramps.

"Why is Stan so mean to his dogs?" asked Seth.

Gramps squinted at the sky. "Stan wasn't always like this," he said. "I met him when I was dating your Gran. He was quiet and shy then. I think he had his eye on her as well. Then most of us got called up to serve in the Viet Nam War. I had some medical training, so I was stationed at Da Nang Air Force Base as a medic. He went into the jungles and fought hard to stay alive."

Gramps pushed a hand through his hair. "He was never the same after he got back. Seemed hardened somehow. Men like him sometimes like to control vicious animals to convince themselves that they're brave and tough."

A hard lump filled Seth's throat as he pictured all the dogs in Stan's yard. He looked down at Prissy who trotted by his side; her tail swinging back and forth in a lazy rhythm. "What if the sheriff says he can have Prissy back?"

Gramps dropped an arm over Seth's shoulders. "I doubt that Sheriff Keller will let him have her back after what he saw today."

"What about all those other dogs? What's going to happen to them?"

The sheriff will probably confiscate the dogs and turn them over to a rescue agency. They'll try to rehabilitate them and find good homes for them."

"What if they can't be rehabilitated?"

"Then they'll have to be put down."

A heavy lump swelled in the pit of Seth's stomach.

They walked in silence till they reached a small square building with a sign in the window that said, "Little Paws Animal Clinic."

Cool air blew on Seth's face as he and Gramps stepped through the door. A woman with curly blonde hair in jeans held a black and white cat in her lap on a bench by the wall.

Gramps and Seth turned to a shiny Formica counter where a young man with light brown hair shooting up from his head in jagged points held a phone to his ear.

"O.K. 2:30 on Thursday. See you then." After writing on a notebook in front of him, he hung up the phone and smiled at Gramps and Seth. "Is it time for Riley's rabies shot?"

"No, Tyler," said Gramps, "I'd like Doc Bradley to look at a different dog today, if she has a minute."

Tyler stood up and looked over the counter at Prissy. "We have an immunization to take care of, if you can wait."

"Sure," said Gramps. He and Seth took a seat next to the window and looked out.

Tyler came around the counter and nodded to the woman with the cat. "You can bring Jinx back now." She followed him through a door at the end of the room.

"Might as well stop and get haircuts while we're in town," said Gramps, eyeing the barbershop across the street.

Seth reached up and tugged on his bangs.

"So is Stan one of the dog fighters you were trying to catch two years ago?" asked Seth.

"The sheriff thinks so, but just because a man owns pit bulls doesn't mean he's guilty of anything. He needs to catch him and the rest of the gang red-handed."

"You mean someone has to see them holding a dog fight?"

"Yep. A reliable witness."

A few minutes later, Tyler walked into the room. "Doctor Bradley will see you now," he said.

They followed Tyler into a room that smelled of disinfectant with a metal table in the middle. Jars of cotton balls and swabs lined the wall on top of a cabinet.

A woman in a white coat opened the opposite door while looking at a clip board. She was thin with green eyes and creases in her forehead. Her chestnut hair curled in just above her shoulders. She looked up and extended her hand with a smile.

"Hi Clint," she said. "How are things up on the mountain?"

"Good, Liz," said Gramps, taking her hand. My grandson here is visiting for the summer."

The vet smiled at Seth. "Is this your dog?"

"Yes. I mean no…" stammered Seth.

"We found her up near my place," said Gramps. "She was in bad shape. We think she has been neglected."

"Alright, let's have a look."

She pulled on some latex gloves and squatted by Prissy. She looked into her eyes and ears with a pen light. Gently pressing her fingers in on the side of Prissy's mouth, she opened the dog's mouth and shone the light inside.

Turning to Seth, she said, "Can you hold her while I take her temperature? She might not like it."

Seth held Prissy's head still while the doctor finished the exam. After probing her sides and moving her hands up and down the dog's legs, the vet lifted a paw and said, "See these cracks between her toes? She has done some serious digging and traveled a good distance before you found her."

"That is probably how she escaped from her previous owner," said Gramps.

Dr. Bradley stood up and took off the gloves. "Looks to be in pretty good shape," she said, "but she's way too thin. And her nipples are enlarged, so it looks like she's expecting. I'm going to give her an anti-bacterial injection and some ointment for her paws. You'll have to follow up with some oral medication." She left the room and returned in a few minutes with a syringe.

"Hold on to her," she said to Seth, as she expertly delivered the medicine. Straightening up, she said, "Bring her back in if she stops eating or starts acting listless."

Prissy's toenails clicked on the tile floor and her tail waved in a floppy arc as she followed Seth and Gramps back into the lobby. Seth looked out the window as Tyler filled out a receipt and put a bottle of pills and tube of medicine into a small sack and handed it to Gramps.

The hair on Seth's scalp prickled. Stan Juke was standing in front of the barber shop talking to the bald guy from the gas station. He stiffened and put his hand on Gramps' arm. Gramps looked up from the receipt and followed Seth's gaze to the men across the street. He put some bills on the counter and held out his hand for change without taking his eyes off the two men.

"Thanks," he said, stuffing the change into his pocket while picking up the bag of medicine. "Let's go out the side door." He draped an arm over Seth's shoulders and guided him out to an alley between buildings. Outside, he whispered, "You have better ears than I do, see if you can get close enough to hear what they're saying." He pointed toward the street.

Seth swallowed.

"Stay, Prissy," he whispered, holding up his hand.

He pressed his back into the building and scooted along the wall till he was near the corner. Looking back at Gramps and Prissy, he hesitated. The old man waved him forward.

Leaning out a little, he heard voices mumbling but no distinct words. A car pulled up to the curb and he took a step backwards. Peeking around the corner, he watched a man with a dog wearing a plastic cone on its head get out of the car and go into the vet's office.

Bending over, he scampered over to the car and hunched behind it, holding his breath. Crouching behind the car, he carefully peered over the hood at the two men.

"Clint Bowman is too nosey for his own good," said Stan.

"Don't worry about Bowman," said Cal. "If he gets too close, I'll take care of him."

Electricity shot up Seth's spine.

"But he could cause us all kinds of trouble if he finds out the fight is near his place," whined Stan.

"No, we can't change the location again," said Cal. "Just see to it that you get the word out that we're moving the date of the fight up."

With that, the big man looked cautiously back and forth. Then he hurried off down the street, leaving Stan Juke staring down at the sidewalk.

Chapter 11

"Sit," said Seth. He held his hand palm facing outward towards Prissy.

She quickly lowered her backside onto the grass.

Quiet settled around Seth like a warm blanket, interrupted only by sounds of clanking mixed with Gramps' tuneless whistle floating out of the garage. Gran threw chicken feed onto the ground from a tin cup in her hand as the hens raced to fill their stomachs.

"Good dog," said Seth. He held out a morsel of fried trout from the night before.

The dog took the fish from his outstretched hand in her teeth and gulped it down without chewing. She stared at Seth without blinking and eagerly licked her chops.

Just then Riley dashed out of the trees with his worn tennis ball in his mouth. Seth's arm felt like it might fall off if he threw it one more time. The slobbery dog dropped it and jumped up on Seth's chest, sniffing his shirt.

"OK, Riley," Seth said, "You can have some too." He held a piece in the air. Riley jumped up and took the meat neatly from Seth's hand.

"OK. Shake." Seth put his right hand out to Prissy.

Riley pushed in front of Prissy.

"No, Riley. Wait your turn."

Riley sat down and tilted his head to the side.

"Shake," he said turning toward Prissy.

Prissy smelled the hand for scraps and licked his fingers.

"No, silly. Shake. Like this." He lifted her right paw and shook it. Then he handed her another small piece of meat. After repeating the action about ten times, Prissy lifted her paw automatically.

"Good girl!" said Seth.

Riley threw himself on the ground and rolled over. Then he bounced up and looked at Seth expectantly.

Seth laughed. "Alright. Here you go." He handed a piece to the one eared dog.

"Seth, can you come here a minute?" asked Gramps' voice from the garage.

Seth divided the last of the fish into two pieces and threw it to the two dogs. They each caught it easily and gulped it down.

Seth walked into the garage where the truck hood was propped open, and Gramps was bending over the engine.

"Can you jump in and turn the motor on?"

Seth looked at the driver's side door.

"Key's in the ignition." Gramps said, without taking his eyes off the metal parts inside the truck.

Seth opened the door and slid up onto the seat. He had never driven or even started a car before. But how hard could it be? He found the key and turned it.

Nothing happened.

Seth looked at all the gauges. Should he push or pull something?

Gramps' face appeared at the open window. He opened the door.

"You've never driven." It wasn't a question.

Seth shook his head.

Gramps pointed to the floor. "Put your left foot on the clutch – that pedal – and push it all the way to the floor." Seth pushed it down. "Hold it in and put your right foot on the brake – that one." He pointed. Seth pushed. "Now turn the key," Gramps said.

Seth turned it and smiled in surprise as the engine growled to life.

Gramps nodded and leaned in. Yelling over the sound of the idling engine, he said, "Now, when I tell you, I want you to put your right foot on the gas pedal there," he pointed again, "and rev the engine." He took a step and then turned back. "Don't let the clutch up, whatever happens, OK?"

Seth nodded solemnly.

After a minute, Gramps yelled, "OK. Give it some gas!" Seth pushed the gas pedal. The engine went from purring to roaring in an instant. Vibrations came up through the seat and rattled his teeth. He pushed hard on the clutch to make sure it stayed down. He heard Gramps yelling but couldn't make out what he was saying.

In a moment, the old man was standing by the truck window.

"You can turn it off now," he yelled, wiping his hands with a dirty rag.

Seth turned off the motor. The sudden silence rang in his ears.

"Alright, scoot over, and we'll head down to the Gas-N-Go for some oil. He slammed the hood down.

Behind him, Gran walked into the garage.

"You can go off and have your fun after you turn the garden soil for me like you promised." She walked in and picked up the shovel from its place by the wall.

Gramps looked sheepishly at Seth. "Be right there," he said over his shoulder as Gran walked out and turned toward the back of the house. Then he turned to Seth. "How about you take your backpack and ride your bike down to the Gas-N-Go and pick up a quart of oil?" He took the wallet from his back pocket and took out a few dollars "Just tell Ted I need a quart of 10-40 weight. He'll know what to give you. You might as well buy yourself a candy bar or something while you're there too." He handed the money to Seth.

"Thanks!" said Seth. He took the dollars from Gramps hand and stuffed them into his back pocket.

Seth gulped in lung-fulls of fresh air as he pedaled as fast as he could down the road. Riley and Prissy kept up easily, running along beside the bike.

He skidded into the gas station and flung a leg off the bike, riding the last few yards hanging on one side. Breathing hard, he jumped off and steered the bike up to the station and leaned it against the wall. Riley and Prissy plopped down next to the bike panting.

The bell on the door jingled as he opened it and walked in.

"Be right with you," said Cal's voice from the garage.

Seth looked around. Ted was nowhere in sight. He pushed down the feeling of panic that rose in his chest. He was pretty sure he had not been seen listening in that day in front of the barber shop, but he didn't like being alone with Cal. He tried to act casual as he peered at the row of candy and chips, but a bead of sweat popped out on his forehead.

He felt, rather than saw, the big man standing beside him.

"My Gramps needs a quart of oil," he said, turning to look up into the dark eyes that stared back like flint above the frowning mouth.

Cal's eyes darted to the big window. When he saw there was no truck by the gas pump, he looked back at Seth and seemed to be sizing him up.

"I've got the money," Seth said, digging in his back pocket.

Cal chewed the side of his cheek for a moment, then he said, "OK, hold on." He went to the lines of yellow cans stacked up in front of the window. "Ten-forty weight?"

"Yes." Seth chose a Snickers and walked over to the cash register.

"That it?" Cal asked, setting the can on the counter next to the cash register with a clunk.

Seth dropped the candy bar next to the oil and fingered the dollars in his hand.

"Nine-fifty," said Cal. He looked out the window again with an impatient glare.

Seth quickly handed over a ten.

Cal opened the cash register, put the bill in the drawer that jutted out and scooped out two quarters. He tossed the money on the counter and slammed the register with a ching.

Seth scraped the coins off the counter and dumped them into his pocket as fast as he could. Then he picked up the oil and candy bar and hurried out the door. Outside, he fumbled with the zipper to his backpack and shoved the oil and candy into it. As he took hold of the handles of the bicycle, his eyes went to the big man inside the store.

Cal was standing by the far wall watching Seth while holding a phone receiver up to his ear.

Chapter 12

Seth swung his leg over the bike and shot out onto the road. The dogs jumped to their feet and joined excitedly in the race. He had just turned the first corner when he heard a motor coming up behind him. He steered to the side of the road to let the vehicle by.

Instead of going around, it slowed and followed closely behind. Turning his head, Seth saw a white truck. His heart pounded in his ears as he recognized Stan Juke at the wheel.

He stood up on the pedals and pushed hard. The truck pulled even with him and the passenger side window rolled down.

"Hey!" Stan yelled. "Let's talk about the dog!"

Seth's lungs burned as he tried to pedal faster.

"Give her back and I'll let you have one of her next litter of puppies!" shouted the man.

"No!" shouted Seth over the sound of the motor. His legs shook as he pushed them in desperate circles.

Stan gunned the truck and zoomed past Seth, causing the tires to kick dirt and dust into the young man's face. Seth coughed and watched the truck climb the hill in front of him, then turn and stop, blocking the road.

Seth's heart beat hard against his ribs when the older man stepped out of the truck and began calling to Prissy.

"Come here, girl," Stan yelled, pointing to the ground next to him.

Spotting a small opening in the trees, Seth jerked the bike off the road and tore into the bushes. "Come Prissy!" he shouted over his shoulder in a raged voice. Both dogs turned instantly and followed him through the leaves.

Dodging boulders and trees, Seth rode crazily away from the road. His white knuckles grasped the handlebars in a death grip as he tried to keep the bike upright while bouncing over dead branches and rocks. Twigs reached out and scratched his face with sharp fingers.

He had no idea where he was going, but knew he had to get as far away from Stan Juke as possible. The bike flew into a sudden dip in the ground and the tires skidded sideways throwing Seth to the ground. Dirt and gravel ripped at his face and arm as he was dragged to a sudden stop.

"Ow," he said, lifting the bike off him and pushing it away. Prissy ran to him and licked his face. He reached for the dog and hugged her to him.

"Good girl," he said into her fur.

Bloody scratches lined his arms like red pen marks. Prissy licked the injured skin.

"I'm O.K.," he told the dog, a little shakily. He pulled off his backpack and looked around. Where was Riley?

Kneeling behind a bush, he put his arm around Prissy and watched for any sign of Stan coming after them. Hearing nothing, he dragged his backpack over to a tree and leaned against the trunk.

Keeping an eye on the bushes he had crashed through; he fished out the smashed Snickers and peeled back the wrapper.

"Sorry, you can't have any," he told Prissy as she eagerly sniffed the candy bar. "It would make you sick." After licking the last of the chocolate off the wrapper, he pulled Prissy close and buried his face in her fur.

Chapter 13

Seth awoke with a start.

The sound of rowdy barking echoed in his head.

"What?" he asked, looking around, confused. It was dark and chilly. He hugged his arms. Something soft and heavy lay on his lap. Then it all came back to him. The bike, the truck. His mad dash into the trees.

The barking came nearer. Then all at once Riley burst into the clearing and pounced on Seth, licking his face with gusto. Prissy jumped up and joined in the barking, dancing around in circles.

"Ugh! Riley!" he said, crossing his arms in front of him.

"Good dog, Riley," said Gramps' voice. The light of a flashlight scanned Seth from head to toe. He sighed with relief. "Next time, if you want to go camping, let me know and we'll bring the tent," he said.

***

"Do you think we ought to call the sheriff?" asked Gran.

Seth wrinkled his nose as she dipped her fingers in a jar of foul-smelling ointment and smeared it onto the scratches on his face and arms. His torn shirt sat in a wad on the kitchen table next to his chair.

Gramps pressed his lips into a thin line. "Sheriff Keller will want to know about this, sure, but Stan will just claim he wasn't anywhere near here today. We don't have any proof and it'll be our word against his."

Prissy jumped up and sniffed Seth's face. When a glob of the ointment dripped onto her nose, she snorted and backed into the corner of the kitchen wiping at her snout with her paw.

"I think I'll just go on down and have a conversation with Stan myself," said Gramps, picking up his keys.

"Clint...," said Gran.

"No harm in just talking, is there?" He stalked out the back door and let it slam behind him.

Gran shook her head. Then she looked up with a start as if she had just remembered Seth. "I'll bet you are hungry," she said, wiping her hands on a towel. "Why don't you go on up and change into some clean clothes while I feed the dogs, then I'll heat up your supper."

"This was my last clean shirt," Seth said, looking at the wad next to him.

"I'll get you one of Gramps' shirts to wear while you wash your clothes." She opened a cupboard. "You can give the dogs some food and water while I see what I can find." She pointed to the big bag of dog food and hurried away.

Seth found a scoop in the bag and filled the bowls to overflowing. Riley and Prissy greedily gulped down the kibbles as he filled their water dishes to the brim and carefully put them on the floor.

"I think this will work," said Gran, coming into the kitchen. She held up a yellow knit top with tiny red roses all over it.

Seth's eyes widened.

"I'm sorry, but nothing in Gramps' drawer is even close to your size," she said, holding out the dainty shirt. "It's just for a couple of hours till your own shirts are clean."

Seth gulped.

Before he could object, Gran threw the shirt on over his head and yanked it down. Seth pulled it away from his skin as if it were on fire.

She smiled and nodded. "That'll work." She took a pan out of a cupboard and put it on the stove.

Seth lurched up the stairs two at a time to scoop all his dirty clothes off the floor. He clambered back down a minute later with sleeves and legs trailing behind, only stopping for a second to pick up a sock that fell to the floor.

***

By the time Seth heard the truck pull up outside, he was relieved to have his own shirt back on, though it was still a bit damp. He lay on his stomach on the rug reading a book called *Tuck Everlasting*. He had finished *The Hatchet* the night before.

He sat up as Gramps walked into the living room followed by Gran. She was chasing him with her jar of smelly ointment.

"I'm fine!" Gramps protested as he held out his arms and backed away from the determined woman. A swollen red cut hung just below his right eyebrow.

"You sit down and let me put this on it, or I'll have Seth hold you down!" said Gran, sticking out her bottom lip.

Gramps gave Seth a look that made it clear that wasn't going to happen if he had a breath in his body; but all Seth could think about was getting as far away from Gran's smelly injury remedy as he could.

"I need to take Prissy out," he said jumping to his feet. Then he left the house as quickly as he could.

Chapter 14

Seth cast his line over the water with a zing where it landed near the middle of the lake with a satisfying plop.

The week before, Sheriff Keller had deputized Ted and Gramps at the courthouse so they could keep an eye on the road and the abandoned cabins around Hidden Lake. Each day they fished different holes while watching for any sign suspicious activity.

Today Gramps and Seth had taken up a spot in a small stand of trees near the Ferguson Cabin. Gramps had propped his pole against a pile of rocks and was leaning against one of the trees with his baseball cap pulled over his eyes. Sparkles of sunlight shimmered on the water and soft breezes flicked the leaves back and forth over their heads.

Prissy lay contentedly at Seth's feet with her feet on her front paws and her eyes closed. Like Gramps, she was enjoying an afternoon snooze.

Splashing in a puddle behind a big boulder, Riley was jumping up and down and biting at something. He bent down and picked it up in his mouth and jerked his head back and forth. Then he brought the mangled creature and laid it at Seth's feet. It was a frog – or used to be a frog. Dead now. He sat back and looked at Seth proudly.

"Mmmm. Thanks," muttered Seth. "That looks delicious."

As Seth started reeling his line in, Riley dashed off into the nearby bushes barking maniacally. Now what?

Seth leaned his pole against a tree and followed the dog into the shrubs. Riley was yapping happily and wagging his tail at a small animal a few feet in front of him. The creature was hunched and covered with pointy barbs. Seth had never seen a live porcupine before, but he knew one when he saw it.

"No, Riley! Get back!" Seth ordered. For a smart dog, Riley was pretty stupid sometimes. Gramps had told him that just last summer he had to take the dog into town to get a bunch of quills pulled out of his snout.

Riley gave Seth a disappointed look, then barked one more time at the prickly animal and sat back on his haunches, sulking.

"Go on." Seth said to the porcupine, "Get moving." He picked up a rock and threw it in the general direction of the animal. The porcupine gave Seth a haughty look, and then waddled slowly away.

As the porcupine disappeared into the bushes next to a massive tree, Seth noticed a rope dangling from one of its thick branches.

"Hey, cool," he said. He walked over and pulled on the rope, staring up into the tree as he yanked on it. Shading his eyes with his hand, he stared out over the lake. This must be the swimming hole Gramps had told him about.

He jumped up and caught the rope with both hands high above his head and swayed back and forth.

With a smile, he held the rope tightly, ran back and swung way out over the water then back. After several wide arcs, he kicked his shoes off and launched himself into the water. The cool water covered him and bubbled up around his ears. He came up laughing and spitting.

Hearing a splash, he looked up to see Prissy in the water paddling hastily toward him. When she reached him, she grabbed his shirt sleeve in her teeth and began pulling him toward shore.

"No! Prissy!" he sputtered. "I'm not drowning!"

He felt his sleeve rip as he pulled his arm away from her. *There goes another shirt,* he thought. He splashed water in her direction and kicked away from the shore.

Rolling onto his back he let the cool water flow over him. A couple of birds flew high overhead and landed on a tree branch. As he flipped onto his stomach and stretched his arms out, he heard a distant thrumming. Water dripped in his eyes as he focused on the sound.

Gramps stood up and motioned to Seth. He swam toward the shore with Prissy right beside him. As he climbed out of the water and stood dripping next to Gramps, the dog shook vigorously from head to foot, leaving the old man nearly as wet as he was.

Holding a finger to his lips, Gramps pointed toward the road.

A truck was coming slowly through the trees.

Gramps and Seth crouched down and watched as a white pickup truck pulled up to the cabin. Two doors opened and slammed shut as Stan Juke and Cal got out.

They crunched on the gravel in front of the old cabin and stopped. Stan's left eye was swollen shut and was a strange black and green color. His bottom lip looked as if a bloated worm had crawled onto his face and died there.

"I don't like being so close to Clint Bowman's place." Stan said through bruised lips.

"That old man? He couldn't punch his way out of a paper bag," said Cal.

Stan turned and gave his friend an angry glare.

"I'll make sure he doesn't get in our way," said Cal.

The hairs on the back of Seth's neck prickled.

"Anyway, tonight is perfect," said the big man. "The sheriff is in White Fish taking care of some poachers down there so there's no one to cause trouble."

Seth rubbed his arms as goosebumps sprang up on them.

Just then Riley ran up to them and laid a stick at Seth's feet.

"What was that?" asked Stan.

"Nothing," said the other man.

"I'm telling you, I heard something over there." Stan scanned the tree line.

Cal moved toward the cabin. "Let's make sure everything is set for tonight," he said.

Stan took one more look around and followed Cal up the wooden stairs.

"Do you think you can find your way home?" whispered Gramps.

Seth nodded.

"OK," the old man looked back at the cabin, then turned to Seth. "Follow the lake around till you come out on the road by our fishing hole. Take the dogs with you.

Riley knows the way. Don't let anyone see you. I'm going to stay here till they come back tonight."

Seth hesitated.

"Tell Gran I'll be home late."

Gramps turned back to the cabin and put his hand behind him waving Seth away.

The sun hung low in the sky by the time Seth came into the yard with the dogs on his heels. Gran looked up from feeding the chickens.

"Gramps is going to be late," Seth said breathlessly.

She nodded. "We'll save him some supper." Then her eyes went to his clothes.

Seth looked down at his damp pants and torn shirt. Without another word, he raced into the house and up the stairs to change.

Chapter 15

The next morning, Gramps' chair was still empty when Seth came down for breakfast.

"He came in around three in the morning," Gran said, lifting the frying pan from the stove. "I expect he'll want to sleep in a bit." She spooned some scrambled eggs and bacon onto two plates and set them on the table.

Just as she was sliding into her chair, a loud pounding came from the front door.

"I'll get it," said Seth. He grabbed a piece of bacon and jumped up. Casually taking a bite, he swung open the front door.

Standing in front of him with his mouth stretched into a smile, was Cal. The man seemed even bigger than Seth remembered him and filled the doorway.

Seth froze.

"Your Grandpa here?" asked the big man. He looked over Seth's shoulder into the room behind him.

Anger radiated through Seth's body. He may not be as big as Cal, but he was as tall, and there was no way he was going to let him hurt Gramps. Before the big man could react, Seth shot behind him and hooked his arm around his neck. Squeezing as tight as he could, he cried, "You leave my Grandpa alone!"

Cal's fingers clawed at Seth's arm and he croaked, "No… I…"

Gran came out of the kitchen wiping her hands with a towel.

"What in the world!" she gasped as she watched Seth and Cal lurch around the porch.

"He's after Gramps!" Seth wailed. The man staggered around, trying to pry Seth's arm from his neck.

Just then a jeep pulled up in front of the house.

"He came here to hurt Gramps!" Seth yelled, as Sheriff Keller and Ted leaped out of the vehicle.

Cal continued to cough and sputter.

The sheriff held up a hand. "Alright, son, you can let him go."

Cal bent over and took in huge gulps of airs and rubbed his neck as Seth let go and stepped back.

"You OK?" Ted asked the big man.

Cal wheezed and nodded his head. "I think so," he rasped.

Sheriff Keller smiled. "Well, I'm sure glad you're on our side!" he said to Seth. "But you don't need to worry about Cal. Can we come in for a minute?"

"Come on in and have a bite to eat," said Gran. She led the way to the kitchen.

Seth kept a wary eye on Cal as the men pulled chairs out and sat around the table.

Gran dished up mounds of eggs and bacon to the men.

"So, as I was saying," the sheriff said to Seth, "Cal here was working undercover for us to catch those dog fighters." He shoveled a bite of eggs in his mouth.

"But I saw him calling someone that day I was at the gas station and then Stan tried to run me off the road," Seth said, pulling out another chair.

Cal took a bite of bacon and said around it, "I knew Stan was coming up the mountain that day and when you showed up, I tried to call him to talk him into coming up later. But he didn't answer. He was already on his way."

Seth studied the big man. "Is that why there were bales of hay inside the cabin?" he asked.

Cal nodded.

"They use them to make a ring for the dogs to fight," said Ted as he took another bite of fluffy eggs. "Mmm." *Swallow* "Thanks Lou. You're the best cook in the state."

Just then Gramps walked into the kitchen, stretching his arms out to his sides.

"Thought I heard a party going on," he said, pushing a hand through his hair.

"Come have some breakfast," Gran said, adding another plate to the table.

When the food was gone and everyone was sitting around holding their stomachs, the sheriff wiped his lips with a napkin and turned to Gramps. "We need you to come down to Kalispell to testify at the County Courthouse next month."

Gramps rubbed his chin. "Is there any way my testimony can be delayed till the end of the summer? I've got my grandson here…"

"Bring him with you. Flathead Lake has some of the best fishing in the state. Bring Lou too. She deserves a vacation."

"Will Stan go to jail?" asked Seth.

"Possibly," said Keller. "It depends. The judge may only fine him since it is his first offence."

"What about all his dogs?" Seth asked.

"We've contacted a rescue agency," answered the sheriff. "They'll find homes for as many as they can." His eyes went to Prissy as she gobbled her dog food. "All except one fine looking Staffordshire terrier. Do you think we could find anyone who might be interested in adopting her?"

Seth's face split into a wide grin.

Chapter 16

"It's a two-hour drive into Kalispell," Gramps said that night as he slid a checker from one square to the next. "I'll have to stay down there till they call me to testify. That could take several days – even a week or two."

"Sorry, Clint, I need to keep an eye on the chickens," said Gran. "Plus, the green beans are about ready to pick, and I don't want them to get too ripe." She turned the page of the book in her hand.

Gramps turned to Seth. "How about you? Want to take a run into Kalispell for a few days? There might be a net down there you could use for your phone game."

Seth reached down and caressed Prissy's soft head. She was getting rounder every day. "Would we take the dogs with us?"

Gramps shook his head. "No, we'll have to leave them behind. We'll be staying in a hotel until the deposition."

"Sorry, Gramps." Seth looked down at the Prissy's swollen belly. "She might need me."

Gramps gave a short nod. "Probably for the best," he said. "You can stay here and help your Gran."

***

When Gramps had been gone for a week, Prissy began pacing around the kitchen restlessly ignoring the morsel Seth slipped her under the table.

Gran studied the caramel-colored dog.

"Let's make Prissy a bed in front of the fireplace," she said. She filled Riley's food and water bowls and told the dog, "You stay in here."

She went to the laundry room and came back with some soft rags and towels. "Make her a bed with these," she said, handing them to Seth. "I think she's ready to have her puppies."

Seth arranged the rags neatly on the floor, but Prissy pawed them into messy piles. Then she lay down and looked at Seth with soft brown eyes. Seth sat on the couch tapping his knees with his fingers.

"Do we need to do something to help her?" he asked.

"She'll know what to do," Gran answered. She sat down by Seth and reached for her guitar. She began playing a soft melody while Seth fidgeted with the fringe on a sofa pillow.

"Here," said Gran, handing him the guitar. "Music relaxes animals – and people."

"I don't know how to play."

"First, sit up tall on the edge of the couch. Rest the guitar on your leg and put your left hand under the neck – don't grab on but make a "V" with your thumb and pointer finger – good." She rested her hands on his shoulders till he lowered them.

"Now, you make different chords by putting your fingers on the right strings." She guided his fingers. "Put your pointer finger here and your other fingers here and here. This is a 'G' chord."

Seth's hand felt like an awkward claw.

"Not so stiff."

He loosened his fingers.

"That's better."

Seth strummed the chord. He realized he was holding his breath and let it out in a whoosh.

Prissy whimpered.

She turned around several times and lifted herself on her haunches. Finally, a tiny wet brown and white blob emerged beneath her. She vigorously licked the gooey creature until the animal gave an exasperated squeak. Then the puppy squirmed its way to her side and latched on with gusto.

Seth laid the guitar on the couch and squatted on the floor beside Prissy. He reached out and gently rubbed her side.

"She's gathering her strength," Gran said, "It might be a while before the next one comes."

Twenty minutes later, the puppy protested loudly as the mother dog raised herself to give birth to a brother or sister.

"Make sure she doesn't accidently lay down on that one," said Gran, pointing to the first puppy as Prissy washed the chocolate-colored newcomer with her tongue.

As Prissy finished her ministrations to the second puppy, two more were born in quick succession. She sniffed the two puppies and chose one to work on.

"Help her with that white one," Gran pointed. "It needs to be stimulated in order to start breathing."

"What do I do?"

"Pick up a towel and carefully rub the membrane off the face."

Seth gulped. He had not realized birth involved so much *ooze*. Seth lifted the tiny limp body as if it were made of glass and rubbed the white face and stomach with the corner of a towel.

"Hold its head a little lower than the body to let the fluids drain."

Seth continued rubbing until at last the tiny puppy gave a satisfying high-pitched squeal.

"Good, now help it get in there to nurse," Gran said. "Don't let the others push it away."

Another hour ticked by. Prissy lay on her side with her eyes closed while the four puppies pressed themselves into her belly pawing at the towels on the floor.

Seth smiled at the greedy animals.

"I think that's it," Gran said, closing her eyes and laying her head against the back of the couch. In a few minutes a soft whistling sound came from her partly open mouth.

Chapter 17

Seth spent the next two weeks practicing moving from chord to chord on Gran's guitar while watching the puppies wrestle and tumble over each other.

"That's starting to sound pretty good," said Gran, coming down the stairs. She smiled at the wiggly bodies on the towels in front of the fireplace. "I think I'll throw together some beef stew for supper tonight, how does that sound?"

"That sounds great!" Seth said. Everything Gran made was yummy.

"Good, you can help peel and chop some potatoes."

Seth jumped up and followed her into the kitchen.

Riley sat at Gran's feet watching her hopefully as she quickly cut the meat into small cubes and added them to a big pot of broth. "Gramps called this afternoon," she said. "They will finish deposing him tomorrow or the next day, and he'll head home right after that."

Gran moved around the kitchen adding herbs and ingredients like a carefully choreographed dance.

Seth nodded as he peeled the potatoes. He was going to miss Gran's cooking.

"Good work," Gran said when he had chopped the potatoes into jagged chunks. "Now you can stir this and

keep it from scorching while I go out and collect the eggs."
She handed him a big spoon and wiped her hands on her
apron as she headed out the back door.

Seth breathed in the tantalizing smells coming from
the pot as he stirred the stew. Maybe he would try to
remember how to make this for his mom when they
got home.

In a moment, Gran was back at the door with a
flushed face.

"The fence broke again!" she said breathlessly. "Help
me round up the hens!" She disappeared from the doorway
and Riley sprang out of the house after her, barking
ferociously.

Seth raced outside to see chickens clucking and running
in all directions.

"Put them in the coop and shut the door!" Gran said,
as she hurried after several birds that were headed for the
trees.

Seth stretched his hands out in front of him and ran
toward the hens, but they scattered before him like a cloud
of clucking feathers. He scanned the yard for something to
use to corral them. Some kind of net.

In a flash, he raced to the garage and grabbed the
fish net off its hook. Back in the yard, he dropped it on
the nearest chicken, scooped it up and pushed it into the
little wood building. After shutting the door, he went after
another one. In a few minutes, all the hens were collected
in the hen house.

He crouched by the fence and studied the wire. His
eyebrows pushed themselves together. The separations
were too neat and clean to have been pulled apart.

Just then he heard the front door slam. Was Gramps home? He had not heard anyone drive up. He stood and sauntered around the side of the house. As he turned the corner to the front yard, his mouth went dry. A white pickup truck sat in the driveway with the gate open and a cage sitting in the bed. Stan Juke was walking across the front yard carrying Prissy.

Chapter 18

"Put her down," ordered Seth.

At first, Stan looked startled, then his face showed satisfaction.

"Well. You rounded up those birds faster than I expected. But it doesn't matter," he said, walking toward the open tail gate. "Thanks to your Grandpa and that traitor, Cal, I had to pay a hefty fine for dog fighting. So, I'm forced to sell some of my dogs. This one should bring a fairly high price, don't you think?"

A scream tore from Seth's throat. He rushed forward with his fists in tight balls.

Stan dropped Prissy on the tail gate and jabbed an elbow into Seth's stomach.

Seth gasped for breath as he bent over at the waist and clutched his abdomen.

"I'll have her sold before the nosy sheriff even finds out," Stan sneered as he shoved the dog into the cage and closed the latch. "Then it'll be too late." Stan lifted the tail gate and slammed it shut.

As Seth fought the urge to retch and desperately tried to drag air into his lungs, a tawny blur whizzed by him.

In seconds Riley pushed Stan to the ground and stood over him, snarling.

Stan screamed with his hands covering his face. "Don't let him hurt me!" he shrieked.

Seth stumbled toward the truck bed. Holding on to the gate, he sputtered, "Good dog, Riley. Watch him."

Riley sat back and growled at the cowering man on the ground while Seth opened the truck bed and let Prissy out of the cage.

"Come, Prissy," he said, patting his thighs.

She leaped down from the truck bed and stood by Seth's side.

"Stay," Seth said, then moved toward Stan, who was scooting on his backside toward his truck.

"I'll buy you a new cell phone!" Stan whined as rose to his knees and then stood swaying on his feet.

Seth took a step forward and in a quiet voice said, "You can't come on a man's property without his permission."

As Stan opened the driver's side door, he suddenly turned and called, "Come Prissy, come."

A low growl came from the dog's throat.

Stan's eyes popped open, and he jumped into his truck, loudly slamming the door. As he spun out in a cloud of dust, the cage bounced out of the truck and fell open to the ground.

Chapter 19

"How would you like it cut?" asked the white-haired barber. He draped the black plastic sheet over Seth's shoulders and fastened it in back.

"Not as short as my Grandpa's" Seth answered.

The barber smiled. "OK. No military cut today." He turned the chair to face a mirror on the wall over a counter covered with combs and cans of shaving cream. "How about a little off the top and sides?"

Seth nodded.

"Just cut an opening in the front so he can see where he's going, Ben," said Gramps as he leaned back in a wood chair and pulled open a newspaper with the words *Flathead Beacon* on the front.

Ben laughed and started combing and snipping over Seth's head.

"I heard you had some trouble up at your place a couple weeks back."

"Yep," said Gramps. Stan Juke tried to walk off with one of our dogs."

Ben shook his head. Ted Brianholt was in here yesterday and he told me Stan was caught over in Lincoln County trying to sell a bunch of stolen dogs. The word is he's down at the county jail now awaiting trial for theft and attempted burglary – Bend your head down just a bit."

He looked at Seth in the mirror. "So, what have you been up to all summer?"

"I found a great fishing hole at the lake near my grandpa's place," Seth answered. "I ride my bike over there every few days to bring back some trout for supper."

"Mmm. Fresh trout is one of my favorites, too."

"I'll bring you some next time I go."

"That would be great. Thanks," the man smiled.

"Also, my dog had puppies and I have to keep an eye on them all the time, so they don't dig under the fence and get in with my grandma's chickens. She says it makes them stop laying."

"Yeah, I guess chickens don't appreciate dogs in their space."

"She's not too happy when they dig in her garden either."

Ben laughed. "How many puppies do you have?"

"Four. Three boys and a girl."

"That sounds like a handful."

"Yes. Gran says as soon as they're old enough we're going to find good homes for them."

"I might like to adopt one myself. Our dog came up missing a few months ago. – There." He turned Seth back to face the mirror and swept the hair off his shoulders with a small whisk broom. "That look alright?"

Seth studied his image while turning his head right and left. "Yes. Thank you."

"What do I owe you, Ben?" Gramps stood and pulled the wallet out of his back pocket.

"Tell you what," said the barber. "You bring your puppies down here next time you're in town and let me choose one, and we'll call it even."

Chapter 20

A cool breeze blew Seth's hair above his head like a dark brown flag flapping in the wind. The place was quiet without the noisy puppies. He missed them, but the smiles on people's faces as each one was chosen gave him a warm, happy feeling.

He sat on the top step of the porch next to his suitcase listening for the sound of a car motor struggling up the mountain. His hand was sweaty as it gripped the plastic bag full of dog food while his other hand scratched Prissy behind the ears. What if his mom wouldn't let him keep her? Just the thought caused his stomach to twist into knots.

Riley leaped onto the porch with a chewed tennis ball in his mouth. He dropped it at Seth's feet watching him eagerly.

Seth laughed and stood up. "All right, Riley. Go get it." He cocked his arm and flicked the ball into the trees.

The front door opened, and Gramps came out with a lumpy bag in his hands. "I have these extra checkers and this board that nobody is using," he said. "You might like to take them with you." He held them out.

Seth smiled. "Thanks, Gramps." He slid the checkers and board into the outside pocket of his bag.

"I wouldn't be too hard on your friends, though, they probably aren't used to such a challenging game," said Gramps.

"Like you were easy on me?"

"Well…"

Seth laughed. "No. I'm glad you didn't let me win. That made it so much more satisfying when I wiped the board with you last night."

Gramps laughed and stretched his arm over Seth's shoulders. "Yep. You won fair and square."

Gran came outside just as the red Prius crunched up to the driveway. She handed Seth something wrapped in wax paper. "Here's a roast beef sandwich in case you get hungry on the way," she said in a thick voice. He reached out and hugged her.

Seth's mom left the driver's door open as she ran to him and pulled him into a hug.

"Oh, I missed you so much!" She held his arms, squeezing his biceps. "Wow! Someone has been working out!" Her eyes dropped to the light brown dog at his side.

"This is Prissy," Seth said, pleading with his eyes.

His heart stopped as his mom looked at his face and then back at Prissy. After a silent minute, she nodded. He had accepted Mel for her sake, now she would accept Prissy for his.

"Alright." She put her hand out. "Welcome to the family," she said, shaking Prissy's raised paw.

She thanked Gran and Gramps over and over, then opened the car door and Prissy jumped onto the back seat.

Gramps was loading his bag into the back when his mom asked, "Hey, where's your cell phone?"

"Oh, I almost forgot it." Seth ran into the house and pounded up the stairs to his room. Shoving the phone into his pocket without looking at it, he raced back to the waiting car. As he opened the passenger side door, Riley appeared and dropped the ball at his feet.

"Riley, you take care of Gran and Gramps, OK?" he said. He picked up the ball and handed it to Gramps.

Gramps stood like a statue for a minute, then, blinking rapidly, he pulled Seth into a rib-crunching hug. "See you next summer?" he asked.

Seth turned and looked at his mom.

"Of course!" she said.

As the car pulled away, Seth turned and waved till his grandparents were out of sight.